"Michael, what's going on? You're late for your shift at the Crashdown."

"Laurie Dupree just sent me this scrapbook. It's more notes from Laurie's grandfather about his abduction by aliens in nineteen forty-six—a whole *series* of abductions, actually."

Max's brow furrowed as he concentrated for a moment. "Nineteen forty-six? That's the year before our ship crashed."

"You got it," Michael said. "I'm betting it was during one of these abductions that the samples of his DNA were taken and used to . . . make *me*. But it wasn't only *Dupree's* DNA they took. He wrote about seeing others aboard the alien ship, including a little girl and a young newlywed couple. That means that . . ." Michael gestured toward Max.

"The other templates." Max stared at Michael with wonder. Max's human genetic makeup—as well as that of Isabel and Tess—had been taken from other humans, just as Michael's had. But they'd found no clue as to the identities of their human "donors."

"If we can find out who the other three templates are, we might find answers to a whole lot of other questions," Max said, his eyes wide.

"Or we can have an alien and abductee family reunion."

SKELETONS
IN THE CLOSET

ROSWELL™

Read all the books in the new series.
SHADES
SKELETONS IN THE CLOSET
DREAMWALK
QUARANTINE

Also available
LOOSE ENDS
NO GOOD DEED
LITTLE GREEN MEN

And don't miss any books in the series that started it all.
ROSWELL HIGH
#1 THE OUTSIDER
#2 THE WILD ONE
#3 THE SEEKER
#4 THE WATCHER
#5 THE INTRUDER
#6 THE STOWAWAY
#7 THE VANISHED
#8 THE REBEL
#9 THE DARK ONE
#10 THE SALVATION

Available from SIMON PULSE

ROSWELL™

SKELETONS IN THE CLOSET

ANDY MANGELS AND
MICHAEL A. MARTIN

From the television series
developed by Jason Katims

SIMON PULSE
New York   London   Toronto   Sydney   Singapore

First Simon Pulse edition November 2002
™ and © 2002 by Twentieth Century Fox Films Corporation. All rights reserved.

Text copyright © 2002 by Andy Mangels and Michael A. Martin

SIMON PULSE
An imprint of Simon & Schuster
Children's Publishing Division
1230 Avenue of the Americas
New York, NY 10020

The text of this book was set in Berkeley Book.

Printed in the United States of America
10 9 8 7 6 5 4 3 2 1

Library of Congress Control Number 2002107316
ISBN 0-689-85446-3

To Phillip Bozarth and Rebekah Holmes, who have been reading my work for a long time.
—A. M.

To James Richard Martin and William John Martin, two small aliens who fill my life with joy.
—M. A. M.

SKELETONS IN THE CLOSET

PROLOGUE

The Oldsmobile barreled headlong through the night, its headlights casting the only light Darryl Morton had seen for hours along Route 40. As the narrow, curved roadway straightened before him, Darryl glanced toward Christine, who sat beside him. Her head would have been leaning against his shoulder were it not for the seat belt he'd insisted that she wear.

I need to be careful with her, he thought, *in her delicate condition.*

Darryl glanced toward her, letting his eyes linger for a moment on her long, white dress. He noticed then that she was still holding the wedding bouquet, which was already beginning to look the worse for wear. *Mrs. Morton,* he thought, his bride's new name. He shifted his gaze momentarily to her midsection, which was clearly visible in the crescent moon's pale glow. Her slim belly had yet to betray any sign of the new life that was steadily growing within her.

"Eyes on the road, darling," Christine said, smiling. "Dad will be pretty upset if you flip us over into a ditch before we get home to make our announcement."

As he returned his attention to the road that kept unspooling before them, Darryl struggled to return Christine's carefree smile. Soon there could be no hiding the fact that she was carrying his child. But now that they were married, he told himself, there was no longer any need for that.

"Which news should we break to your dad first?" Darryl said with a wry smile. "That we're about to make him a grandfather? Or that we ran off to a little chapel in Las Vegas to tie the knot before anybody found out?"

Another quick glance revealed that her smile had been replaced with a thoughtful scowl. Her expression convinced him that she was finally visualizing the same scene that had been plaguing him all weekend: a tableau of the old man reaching for his shotgun while loudly accusing Darryl of getting his innocent daughter pregnant and dragging her off to be further corrupted in the wretched nest of gambling and gangsters that was Las Vegas.

The old man certainly would be in no mood to hear Darryl's observation that the Flamingo Hotel had seemed far too nice to be connected with mob types, in spite of what the newspapers said.

A long silence, broken only by the rhythmic sounds of tires and the engine, engulfed the car. Faded yellow lines paraded out of the darkness, only to disappear almost instantly beneath the Olds.

After a road sign that read GALLUP 50 MILES whizzed by, Christine interrupted the quiet. "Can you slow down a bit,

Darryl? Maybe we shouldn't be in such a hurry to get home."

Darryl couldn't have agreed more. As he eased his foot off the pedal, he contemplated blowing right past home. They were young and in love, and they had each other. They could start a new life together anywhere they wanted.

Besides, a trip into the complete unknown had to be preferable to dealing with her father when he was at full roar.

As the car came to the crest of a low hill, something up ahead caught Darryl's eye. Christine had obviously seen it as well.

"What's *that*?" she said, her brow furrowing.

Darryl studied the distant point of white light in silence. At first, he thought nothing of it. It had to be the headlight of an oncoming vehicle, maybe a motorcycle, or a car with a burned-out lamp.

Then he noticed that it was floating in the air.

"Maybe it's an airplane," Christine ventured.

"Maybe," he said. But the speed at which it moved and switched directions was like no aircraft he'd ever seen. He wondered if the government might have been testing some secret project way out in the sparsely populated reaches of western New Mexico.

Suddenly, the light began heading quickly toward them, moving like a Japanese "Zero" preparing to strafe Pearl Harbor. Darryl quickly slowed the Olds down and brought the car to a bumpy halt on the deserted road's shoulder before pulling the wheel all the way to the left.

"What are you doing?" Christine said. Darryl heard an edge of fear in her usually sanguine voice.

Darryl did his best to sound calm, in control of the situation. "I'm getting us out of here."

Shoving the transmission into low gear, Darryl lurched the car into an awkward U-turn, then pushed the accelerator down hard. The car fishtailed onto the blacktop, and he struggled to get the vehicle back under control.

Christine turned around and watched the light approaching through the rear window. The reflection in the rearview mirrors was becoming steadily more bright, rising quickly to an almost blinding intensity.

"It's still coming toward us," Christine said, unnecessarily.

Darryl could hear his pulse pounding in his ears, drowning out the strenuous revving of the engine as he slammed the pedal all the way to the floor. He squinted through the gathering brilliance in a vain effort to see the road.

I'm going to get us killed this way, he thought, suddenly releasing the accelerator. His foot stabbed at the brake, and the Oldsmobile quickly skidded to a halt along the roadside.

As the light increased in intensity, flooding the car's interior with golden radiance, a peculiar calm descended on him. Darryl was mildly surprised to note that he no longer felt any fear. Squinting at Christine, he saw that she, too, appeared oddly calm.

Maybe God's decided that after Hitler and Tojo there's been enough history. Maybe it's the Last Days and we're being taken up to heaven.

He felt a bittersweet pang of regret for the unborn child he would now never see.

Darryl noticed that Christine had released her seat belt and opened the passenger-side door. Without even taking the time to grab the car keys, Darryl let himself out the car's other side. Within moments, the couple met at the back of the car, holding hands as they looked into the still-intensifying illumination.

Darryl looked up into the source of the ever-spreading light and saw a large, indistinct shape hovering within it, growing steadily lower and closer. Gauging the thing's size accurately was next to impossible, though it certainly looked quite large against the starkness of the desert night sky.

He turned his gaze to Christine and stroked her long blond hair with his free hand. Her smile told him that whatever was coming held no fear for her. Still holding hands, Darryl and Christine Morton took a step toward the fiercely growing light.

The light washed over them, swallowing them whole.

1

TODAY

"Dude, you got him!" Steve Case playfully punched his friend in the shoulder, unmindful of the fact that his friend still had his finger on the air rifle's trigger.

Monk Pile grinned, just as careless, as he brought the gun down. His dog, Blue, jumped excitedly, until Monk pointed off in the direction of his last shot. "Go get it, Blue!"

As the mutt scampered forward with a growl, Monk wiped the sweat from his brow and scanned the area, alert to any sign of the fleeing jackrabbit's presence. But nothing moved across the expanse of ocher-hued earth, low cholla cacti, and coarse desert grasses of Tenpipe Bluff. Monk and Steve hadn't really been hunting for any real purpose other than just to enjoy the hunt; it was their mutual day off from Meta-Chem Pharmaceutical, and there wasn't much else interesting or fun to do on a day this hot. They'd already seen the summer blockbusters during the afternoon cheap shows at the Cinema 4 and Del Norte

Twin theaters, and neither of them had much on their social calendars at the moment. Graveyard hours at work tended to have a chilling effect on any potential love life.

"Hey, Blue, you missed him!" said Steve, yelling. The dog had run past the downed rabbit, and hopped over a scrub-covered hillock near the edge of the woods, his back paws kicking up sandy earth. Steve looked over at Monk, his face somewhat expectant. "Maybe he smelled something else? Bigger game?"

"I hope it's not another coyote," grimaced Monk. "Last time he tangled with one of those, it cost me darn near two hundred bucks in vet bills." He broke into a languid trot, beckoning for his friend to follow. "C'mon. Let's go see what's got his attention."

The two men climbed the small hill, loose sand and gravel cascading over their scuffed work boots. Monk took a cursory glance at the dead rabbit that lay near the top, smiling for a moment to see that its fur wasn't too badly disfigured by the gunshot. Besides the pelt, the animal's wide, flat feet would be a surefire sale to Skenches, the local taxidermist. *Guess those weren't such lucky rabbit's feet after all,* he thought as they neared the top.

"What you got there, Blue?" Monk asked. The dog was standing with his back to them, growling, and shaking his head back and forth. He was digging frantically into the earth near some trees, and had already created a small depression. Monk could see that his pet had already grasped something in his jaws, a dust-covered object that was sticking out of the hole in the ground. *A gopher?*

A moment later Monk's stomach churned. He realized that what Blue had found was no gopher.

"That's an arm, dude!" Steve exclaimed. As they came closer to Blue, Monk could see that the dog was indeed puling at a human arm. Or at least what was left of it. It was barely more than a skeleton at this point, though for some reason the desert animals had left the heat-shriveled, jerky-like flesh alone. Blue wasn't of the same mind, apparently, and he tugged at the appendage, which protruded from the ground at an odd angle. The shredded remains of a brown-and-white long-sleeved shirt were visible in the dust. What remained of the fabric appeared scorched.

"Blue! Heel!" Monk said, his voice commanding. The dog backed off a bit, circled, then settled into a defensive stance, growling, the hairs along its spine raised and its tail rigid. Monk and Steve crouched, and Monk laid the gun down in the dust. He looked over at his friend. "It's definitely human. And it looks like it's attached to something."

Steve's eyes were wide. "A dead body! Whoa." He reached out as if to touch it, then apparently thought better of it and withdrew his hand. "Should we, you know, dig it up?"

Monk stared at his friend as if he had just arrived from another planet. "No, man. This could be like a crime scene or something. We gotta call Sheriff Valenti." Something in his mind clicked, and he remembered that his brother, a deputy, had told him that Valenti had been replaced a few months ago. "I mean, Sheriff Hanson."

"We'll have to call it in from the CB radio on the truck," Steve said, standing. He looked as if he still wanted to touch the body, but Monk knew he wouldn't.

Monk rose as well and grabbed his gun. Slapping his

leg to signal Blue to follow, Monk stepped to the top of the low hill and prepared to skitter-slide down the slope. "Grab the rabbit on the way down," he called, gesturing to Steve.

Just before moving forward and down, Monk sneaked a final look over his shoulder at the arm, which was still trapped within its dusty grave. From a few yards away, it almost looked like a weird alien plant from some B-grade sci-fi movie. Monk noticed then that the mummified fingers were curled, as if they had been grasping at something when their owner had died. Monk shivered, although the air was warm and dry.

Whose body is this? And why is it buried out here, on the outskirts of Roswell?

2

Max Evans stepped through the back door of the Crash-down Café, into the locker room and prep area. He was always slightly surprised that Jeff Parker didn't keep the door locked—at least during business hours—but maybe he just wasn't inordinately concerned about crime.

The crime rate in Roswell wasn't all that high. Not the *known* crime rate anyhow. Max knew that he and his friends had performed more than their share of illegal acts over the last two years, though he could justify them given that they had generally been committed in the name of self-preservation.

Max moved over to the swinging door that led out to the public area of the Crashdown and he peered through the circular window there. Liz Parker was working, of course—which was his main reason for being there. She was balancing several dirty plates on one arm as she headed back toward the wash area behind the counter. Despite the tired and bored look in her eyes, and the wisps of hair that peeked out from under her alien-themed tiara, he couldn't deny her beauty. Even the awful lime green waitress dress, with its big-headed silver "alien" apron, didn't make her any less pretty, though he certainly preferred her in a tank top and jeans, her black hair floating freely around her shoulders, accenting her dark, almond-shaped eyes.

It hadn't even been two years since Liz had been shot in the abdomen. Max had only an instant to decide whether he would use his alien powers to heal Liz, or preserve his anonymity by letting her die on the cold floor of her family's restaurant.

It hadn't been much of a choice. Max had always had a crush on Liz, and even though he and Michael and Isabel had isolated themselves from romantic contact with normal people—and had made a pact not to use their alien powers in ways that might bring them unwanted attention—his emotions had been wholly human at that moment. He had put his hand on her wound, concentrated, and allowed his essence to merge with hers for a moment.

But that moment had had far-reaching consequences. Max and Isabel and Michael had never allowed anyone to learn that they were really extraterrestrials, and now the number of people who knew the truth of their alien origins—Liz, Maria DeLuca, Alex Whitman, former Sheriff Jim Valenti, his son Kyle—was unnerving. To say nothing of the forces that seemed intent on either exposing or eradicating them. Between the secret military groups first led toward them by the late FBI Agent Kathleen Topolsky, plus Nicholas and the alien Skins, their less-than-friendly duplicate counterparts from New York, and assorted others, the last two years had been fraught with considerable danger.

And then there was Tess, the genetic duplicate of Max's wife on their home world of Antar. Tess's betrayal months ago had been hard on their circle of friends. She had engineered the death of Alex, and had manipulated Kyle and others into moving her plan forward. And then, when her treachery stood revealed, Tess had stolen the Granilith, the craft that would allow her to return to their home planet, carrying within her Max's child—the unborn son of their world's king and the heir to the throne of Antar.

Things hadn't been the same since Tess's departure. Max's future with Liz remained uncertain, though he knew that although Liz still seemed to have feelings for him, the memory of his tryst with Tess wore heavily on her. He tried not to dwell on the matter of Tess too much, but his heart ached for the son he would never see. He was determined to find a way to reach home again, and to see his son.

Almost as if she knew he was there, Liz looked toward the doorway's window and Max. He raised a hand in a sheepish wave, slightly embarrassed at having been caught staring at her. She smiled slightly, then dipped her head away. She spoke to one of the other waitresses behind the counter and headed back in Max's direction.

"Hi, Max," she said simply after she had come through the door.

Max wanted to take her in his arms, kiss her, smooth the unruly shock of hair from her brow. He settled instead for giving her a wan smile, swallowing his more intense emotions. "Hey. I just came by to see how things were going."

"We had a rush earlier, but it's kinda slowed down now," Liz said, gesturing over her shoulder with an upturned thumb. "What about you? Aren't you working at the UFO Center today?"

"Brody had to do something with his daughter this morning, so he decided not to open. He said he might come in later, but gave me the day off if I wanted it." Max shifted his feet and regarded Liz from beneath his dark bangs. "I was hoping you might, you know, be able to take some time off and we could . . . hang out or something. Maybe go to a movie or . . ."

"Oh," Liz said simply. He could see her eyes jagging back and forth, the sign that she was considering fifteen complex answers at once. It was those times when she usually was reduced to one-syllable responses. "Well. Um. Sure. Not now, but later? I'm off at six or so." She turned and looked at a schedule posted on the wall, then turned back, nodding. "Yeah. Six it is. And my schedule just happens to be free."

He grinned widely. "Great. Anything you want to—"

The door to the dining area opened with an abrupt slam and a harried-looking Maria DeLuca launched into the room. She was dressed in the same ridiculous waitress outfit as was Liz. "Liz, do you know where—" She saw Liz wasn't alone and gave Max a cursory glance. "Oh, hi Max." Before he could respond, she turned back to her friend. "Liz, do you know where Michael is? Billy's shift at the grill ended fifteen minutes ago, and he's getting *really* whiny."

"Did you call him?" Liz asked.

Maria rolled her eyes. "*Duh.* Of *course* I called him. But he's probably ignoring my calls. We had a thing last night that—"

She stopped herself, looked at Max, then waved her hands as if to wipe the air clean. "Anyhow, he's not answering."

"I haven't heard from him," Liz said.

"I'll see if I can find him," Max said. He looked longingly at Liz for a moment. Staying with her was preferable by far to managing whatever new trouble Michael may have gotten himself into.

"Oh, that would be great!" Maria said with sarcastic enthusiasm. "Not that I want to interrupt your fumbling stabs at rekindling your epic-but-tragic romance, but we've got a business to run here."

Liz shot Maria a dirty look. Maria put her hand on Liz's arm as she headed them both back toward the door. "Sorry, Liz. I'm just cranky." She turned back to look at Max for a moment. "Why can't you guys have some kind of useful alien communicators implanted in your pecs or something?" Not waiting for his answer, she went back through the swinging door.

Liz shook her head, mortified. Max stepped toward her. "I'll just, uh, go look for Michael then." She looked up at him. Though he badly wanted to embrace her again, he decided instead to leap in another direction. He bent slightly and kissed her forehead. "See you tonight."

As he turned to leave, Max saw a smile light up Liz's face. But knew it couldn't outshine the one that was forming on his own.

Max wasn't surprised when he received no response to his knock. He knew that silence didn't necessarily mean that the apartment was empty; Michael was more than capable of ignoring even an urgent knock at his door, particularly when he was in one of his bleaker emotional funks.

Max placed a hand on the doorknob without turning it. Concentrating for all of a second, he sent a surge of power through his hand and into the knob. It turned in his grasp, as though exercising a will of its own.

Michael Guerin was seated on the couch, his back to the door, papers spread out across the coffee table. "You didn't need to use your powers, Max," he said, without looking. "It wasn't locked."

"Michael, what's going on? You're late for your shift at the Crashdown." Max moved toward the couch, to see what Michael was studying so intently.

"So they sent the king after me to get me to my job flipping burgers?" Michael asked. Max knew that Michael was still having trouble dealing with the recent revelations about their past lives on Antar. Max had been king, and Michael had been his second-in-command and military adviser. But while that arrangement may have worked well on their home world, it was often less than ideal here on Earth. Here they were different people. Literally.

Michael turned, and Max saw he was holding an old photograph and some musty papers. A padded mailing envelope lay on the couch beside him. "Laurie Dupree just sent me this scrapbook. She found it in the mansion with her grandfather's stuff."

Max recognized the man in the picture as Charles Dupree. The yellowed photograph had been made in 1935, but it might as well have been a shot of Michael, taken yesterday. Earlier in the year, they had discovered that Dupree was quite likely the genetic template for the human DNA that Michael carried.

"What is it?" Max asked, momentarily putting aside the situation at the Crashdown.

"More notes from Laurie's grandfather about his abduction by aliens in nineteen forty-seven—a whole *series* of abductions, actually. These weren't in the diaries I got from her before," Michael said, gesturing toward a set of slim volumes sitting on the table amid the papers. "She said these were hidden."

Max's brow furrowed as he concentrated for a moment. "Nineteen forty-seven? That's the same year our ship crashed."

"You got it," Michael said. "These notes were written about six months before the crash. And given what he writes about, I'm betting it was during one of these abductions that the samples of his DNA were taken and used to . . . make *me*."

Max sat down on a nearby chair, his mouth falling open involuntarily. He reached for the papers, and Michael handed them to him. "We knew they got his DNA somehow. And that it had to be either Nasedo or the other alien who actually took the sample. Or, it could have been others on the ship who didn't survive."

"Whoever," Michael said with a shrug. "But it wasn't only *Dupree's* DNA they took. He wrote about seeing others aboard the alien ship, including a little girl and a young newlywed couple. That means that . . ." Michael gestured toward Max.

"The other templates." Max stared at Michael with wonder. Max's human genetic makeup—as well as that of Isabel and Tess—had been taken from other humans, just as Michael's had. But they'd found no clue as to the identities of their human "donors."

"We always knew they were out there," Max said at length. "But we've never had any hard information about them before. Does Dupree say anything specific?"

"No names in this section, just descriptions," Michael said, frowning at the stacks on the table. "There are *other* pages with lots of names on them. And he may have written more pages that are missing from this pile of stuff. It's hard to tell. They're *all* written like he was on drugs or something. It's not a very easy read."

"If we can find out who the other three templates are, we might find answers to a whole lot of other questions," Max said, his eyes wide.

"Right," Michael said dismissively. "Or we can have an alien and abductee family reunion."

Max gave him a sour look. "Let me have a turn going through this stuff. Maybe I can find more information at the UFO Center, if I can get some clues from this as to where to look, or even what it is I'm looking for. Meanwhile, you'd better get to work, or Maria's going to—" Max's cell phone rang, interrupting him.

Max clicked it on. "Hello?" A shrill voice buzzed into his ear. "Yeah, Maria, he was here, but he's already left. He should be there any minute." Another burst of voice, and Max winced slightly. "You tell him that. You'll see him before I will. Yeah. Okay. Bye."

Max looked over at Michael, who was standing up and pulling on a loose-fitting plaid shirt over his T-shirt. "As I was about to say, Maria's pretty pissed off."

"I'm *shocked*, Maxwell," Michael said.

"I'll look into this some more," Max said, holding up a few pages of Dupree's notes.

"Don't take the stuff with you," Michael replied as he stepped toward the door. "I don't want them to accidentally get mixed up with Brody's files or something."

Max nodded, and a moment later Michael was gone. Max settled back in the chair and began reading. The page on top appeared to have been written in a shakier hand than the rest, as if Dupree was extremely agitated when he wrote it. As Max read further, he started to understand why.

Max had found what appeared to be Dupree's written account of his abduction by the aliens. . . .

3

SUNDAY, JANUARY 19, 1947

The world around him was awash in searing white light. Squinting against the glare, Charles Dupree slowly drifted back to consciousness, colored spots capering across his vision. Lying on his back, he felt disoriented, dazzled and stunned by the merciless brilliance.

His first thought was to wonder whether he was dead. But as he gradually became aware of his body, he dismissed the notion. *Ghosts don't have bladders,* he thought. *And I have to piss like a racehorse.*

As his eyes slowly adjusted to the glare, Dupree struggled to turn his head. The air carried a faint but odd aroma, like hot maple syrup mixed with Tabasco sauce. He was determined to take in more of the room in order to find out where he was. His movements were sluggish, labored. It felt as though he were fighting some invisible force that had gained control of his body, forcing him into immobility. *They must have drugged me,* he thought, anger and fear jostling at the forefront of his muddled thoughts.

He paused in his struggles for a moment. Who exactly were "they"? And how had they taken him from that lonely stretch of Route 10 he'd been traversing on his way back to Tucson? He remembered the dark ribbon of roadway that had stretched ahead of him into the desert night. He recalled the hypnotic rhythm of the painted lines as they suddenly appeared beneath his headlight beams and just as quickly disappeared beneath the truck.

Then came the dazzling, searing light. Dupree remembered being startled into a swerve that had gotten Old Rusty up on two wheels for a terrifying, time-frozen instant. He'd come very close to rolling the truck right over before the wheels finally regained contact with the pavement, sending him into a screeching spin. Just as he'd manhandled the vehicle back under control, it mysteriously lost power. The dead truck rolled to a stop on the shoulder, gravel crunching and popping beneath its tires.

Dupree had felt vulnerable inside the stopped truck. It was like the time he'd been trapped behind enemy lines with nothing but a bayonet knife, a nine-millimeter pistol, and two bullets—only this situation was even worse. At least during the war he'd known what he was up against. Here on the roadside, bathed in a mysterious light, he had no idea who or what was after him. Hiding in the all-consuming glare hadn't seemed like a viable option; stepping cautiously outside the truck appeared to be his best alternative, whatever the danger.

He stood on the gravel-strewn shoulder, an arm thrown up across his face to protect his eyes from the brilliance. Squinting over his forearm, he saw that the light was coming from the sky. And that it seemed to be growing steadily more intense.

Seconds later, it engulfed him entirely.

And then he had found himself here. Wherever "here" was.

Now that his eyes had adjusted to the ambient light in the chamber in which he had just awakened, Dupree looked straight up, then shifted his gaze to look left. He saw that he was in a metal-walled room with a high, vaulted ceiling. It was hard to tell precisely where the light was coming from. All he could tell for certain was that this place was like nothing he had ever seen in all his twenty-seven years. In fact, it was hard to believe it was even real.

Great, Dupree thought. *I've been hijacked into the cover of a cheap pulp magazine.*

From the corner of his eye he saw movement. He forced his head to follow it, though it felt like so much lead.

A night-dark silhouette blocked some of the room's light, like a pinhole projection of a solar eclipse. A vaguely human form, visible only as a moving shadow, glided toward him, followed by a second figure. He tried to speak, but his tongue felt too thick and heavy to form words. The shadow-shapes approached him closely, and he felt a sudden bump, as though the surface on which he lay was being moved.

They're wheeling me away somewhere, he thought, wishing he could speak. Or at least get a good glimpse of whoever was moving him across the chamber. Panic warred with hope within him. *Maybe I'm safe. Maybe somebody found me on the side of the road. Maybe this is a hospital.*

But if this place really was a hospital, then why was it that he could hear no one speaking? The only sounds that reached his ears were the gentle whispers of wheels moving across a smooth floor, the small footfalls on either side of him, and an intermittent clicking noise, like cicadas serenading one another on a hot summer night.

The weird quasi-silence stretched as Dupree was wheeled into an adjacent chamber. Still more light, this time from gleaming ceiling-mounted fixtures, assaulted his eyes, forcing him to shut them tightly. Fear and a nearly irresistible desire to flee rose within him as countless small hands bore him from where he lay onto a second hard surface. He wanted to rise, leap to his feat, lash out, run like hell. But his body wouldn't respond.

And still no one spoke.

Dupree tried to get a good look at the room, but now even his eyes refused to respond to his will. Hands moved across his flesh. He felt a sharp jab in his left forearm, then another in his right. An abrupt pain seized his abdomen, then just as swiftly abated. It felt as though something sharp had skewered his right thigh, causing the muscles to cramp and spasm. Something warm touched his temple, gently at first, only to be replaced by a metallic object that felt like a knitting needle heated nearly to its melting point.

The object made a sickening rasp as it suddenly moved, instantly piercing skin and bone. Dupree's mouth opened, his lips forming a scream. But he heard nothing save the busy footfalls of his tormentors, the methodical clatter of their instruments, and those maddening, rhythmic clicking sounds, which began to sound almost like a language he couldn't understand. Were these people communicating in some sort of code?

The pain subsided slightly, and Dupree found that he could open his eyes again. Spots no longer danced before him, and the light levels now seemed almost tolerable. He saw that his body had been strapped to a low table and that his shirt and dungarees were shredded. Long, slender metallic objects pierced his body in numerous places, along his torso, his legs, his arms. A forest of delicate silvery needles surrounded his head.

Through the tangle of weird apparatuses, Dupree watched his captors move. They no longer appeared only as backlit silhouettes, though the metal objects that now surrounded his head made it hard to get a good look at them as they passed before him, going about their obscure business. Because each of them seemed indistinguishable from the others—and because they moved in and out of his view so quickly—he wasn't certain how many of them were present. There might have been four or five of them, or perhaps three times that many, judging from the repetitive clicking sounds he heard coming from points all around the room. He watched the creatures as closely as his almost immobile head allowed, though he could see only their backs as they turned their attention to other parts of the room, clicking who-only-knew-what information back and forth to one another.

Whoever these people were, there was no way they could be doctors. Doctors generally didn't make cricket noises. And doctors usually wore white coats or surgical gowns. But these people seemed to be naked, their wrinkled skin a mottled gray. They were hairless, with heads that seemed too large for their truncated bodies, and long-fingered limbs that looked weirdly slender and overly flexible. At least one of them, he suddenly noticed with a shiver, seemed to be covered from head to toe with a thick coating of a blue, gelatinous goo. His stomach threatened to turn over violently. He closed his eyes tightly until the waves of discomfort passed.

Sideshow freaks, Dupree thought, though he'd never seen their like at any carnival midway. He wanted to scream at them, but discovered that he couldn't make a sound. He heard silence, broken only by a few desultory clicks and the quiet clatter of unimaginable metal instruments. The sounds brought to mind the horrific tortures some of his buddies had suffered at the hands of their Japanese captors during the war.

With an effort that brought a sweat to his brow, Dupree turned his head to the right. He was startled to see that there were indeed other people in the chamber who were recognizably human. He felt a surge of relief, though it lasted only long enough for him to notice that his new-found companions were in no position to help him.

On a low table only a dozen or so feet away from his own lay a young man and a woman, both unconscious and breathing shallowly. They appeared to be in their early or middle twenties, not much younger than he was. The woman was strikingly beautiful, with long blond hair and a physique that might have elicited a wolf whistle from him under happier circumstances. She was dressed in a long white wedding gown, a bouquet of flowers still clutched in her hands, an incongruous sight in this unfriendly place. She looked as though she might be roused by a kiss, like some fairy-tale princess.

The man who lay strapped beside her wore a disheveled black tuxedo, his dark hair tousled across his forehead, revealing his protuberant ears. A look of determination was frozen across his features, as though his captors hadn't succeeded in taking him without a fight.

Like Dupree, both the bride and the groom were festooned with innumerable metal contraptions, needles, and probes of various lengths and sizes. A pair of the gray-backed figures busied themselves checking the ungodly equipment that pierced the couple's bodies in countless places. He tried to shout at them to leave the couple alone. His fists clenched and unclenched in impotent rage. He wanted nothing more than to get his hands around one of their gray, mottled necks.

From the left side of the room, a child's voice cut through the silence like the peal of a small bell. With another exhausting effort, Dupree turned his head in the direction of the sound.

Two other short, gray creatures were shepherding a little girl into the room, ushering her toward another low table. The girl, who couldn't have been more than four or five years old, wore a yellow gingham dress and displayed a beguiling smile. She was a remarkably beautiful child, with blond hair falling about her shoulders in a long, fine cascade. Her hands and knees were grass-stained, as though she'd just been romping in the yard.

The little girl was giggling. *She thinks they're playing,* he thought. Horror left a metallic taste in his mouth.

Dupree's fear quickly gave way to anger. If these freaks thought he was just going to sit idly while they hurt a helpless child, then they had another think coming. *Whatever drugs they pumped me with have to wear off sooner or later. There's got to be a way off this table.*

He noted with no small amount of satisfaction that he seemed to have recovered some control of his body over the past minute or so. Unfortunately, the numerous metal probes piercing his flesh were keeping him effectively pinned to the table. He felt like a butterfly trapped in some demonic bug collector's killing jar.

Dupree watched helplessly as one of the small gray people used its too-long arms to hoist the laughing little girl upward. The creature set her down on the table with surprising gentleness. Another began strapping her to the table.

The child's eyes still held no fear. "Big eyes," she exclaimed, and he noticed that their captors' dark eyes were indeed quite large. Those eyes never blinked, adding to their eeriness. *They must be wearing masks,* Dupree thought.

He turned his eyes to the ceiling, which bristled with gleaming metal armatures identical to the ones that held him and the newlywed couple. Slowly, the armatures lowered a dozen sharp metal lances toward the laughing child. The gray creatures, their faces obscured by the instruments that surrounded Dupree's head, clicked to one another in apparent approval.

No! I have to distract these damned carnies. Dupree opened his mouth and tried to shout a warning to the little girl. He heard a loud but inarticulate cry, and was mildly surprised when he realized that the tortured sounds had come from his own throat.

Dupree tried to shout again, this time with somewhat better control over both lungs and voice. "Get away from her, you bastards! I'll show you where you can stick those needles!"

The echo of his cry lingered for a moment. The clicking abruptly stopped. The little girl ceased her laughter, her eyes as big as saucers.

One of the gray figures turned toward him.

Dupree was exhausted from the effort of shouting, and felt as if his body were melting onto the table like cheese on a hot griddle. But he was encouraged by the fact that he had finally gotten the attention of these people.

He closed his eyes, screwing up his courage. *Maybe I can convince them to release us. Or at least talk them into letting the little girl go. I just have to reach them on some human level.*

Then Dupree opened his eyes and found himself looking directly into the face of one of the small gray men. With only inches separating them, Charles Dupree stared deeply into plum-size eyes as black as an anthracite mine at midnight. And it was no mask, he realized.

The face that regarded him was anything but human.

4

Sheriff Hanson scanned the sky, but no vultures were in sight. He knew it was a silly thought, but Hollywood—and a childhood spent reading pulp cowboy novels—had trained him to believe that when you found a dead body in the desert, there would always be vultures circling above.

The day's heat was likely to be miserable, at least out here on the bluff. Two of his deputies— Lenny Carter and Owen Blackwood—were carefully excavating the remains. Deputy Dina Heikenberry stood nearby, snapping pictures of the entire painstaking procedure. All of them were already sweating profusely in the early sun, wide rings of moisture spreading under their arms and wet patches coursing down their backs like underground streams.

Hanson was vigilant, patrolling the area, alert for any clue to the corpse's origin. The department's dog, a bright-eyed nine-year-old German shepherd named Nanna, was snuffling around the location as well; she wasn't spry enough to be an attack dog, but she certainly had a nose for trouble. So far, neither the dog nor Hanson had turned up any significant information. Although there was a barely used highway turnoff nearby—which probably had been used by whoever dumped the body—time and the inexorable action of the desert elements had long ago erased any trace of either tire tracks or footprints. Even the boot prints of the two young men who had reported finding the body were barely visible.

The sheriff mentally reviewed his notes on the affair. That morning, Monk Pile and Steve Case, two off-duty security guards from Meta-Chem Pharmaceutical, had been hunting rabbits out in the scrub, where they'd found what appeared to be the remains of a human body. They had tried to call in the discovery on their truck's CB radio, but for some unexplained reason, reception was poor in this area. They had driven into town to the sheriff's office, where they had breathlessly told their tale. Then they'd led Hanson and his deputies out to the location of the body.

Although the two men had been eager to offer their assistance, Hanson had told them to go home; he didn't want to risk disturbing whatever evidence might lie in the nearby underbrush and trees by having untrained people tromping around the area unnecessarily.

A dust cloud signaled the impending arrival of another vehicle. Even from a distance, Hanson recognized the sounds of Bill Bender's Jeep. He stepped down a small, dusty slope he had just climbed, half sliding in the gravel, and moved toward the area where the rest of the official trucks and cars were parked.

Bender parked and stepped out of the Jeep. He was a notch shorter than the sheriff, bald but for a fringe of graying hair. He grinned wryly at Hanson. "Morning, Randy. Little early for a coroner call, isn't it?"

Hanson grinned. "Aw, Bill, just 'cause they always do autopsies at night on *The X-Files* doesn't mean we've got to run our operation that way."

Bender opened the back of his Jeep and grabbed a heavy canvas duffel bag marked with the emblem of the Chaves County Coroner's Office. The monogram was a formality, really, since the office consisted of only a handful of people—most of whom actually worked out of the Albuquerque office—but Bender had confided once that he thought the official logo might make any smash-and-grab car thief think twice about trying to lift the bag out of his car.

"So, what have you got for me this morning?" Bender asked.

Hanson gestured in the direction of the spot where most of the deputies were working, over a nearby rise. "Couple of guys were hunting rabbits and found an arm sticking out of the ground this morning. Looks pretty badly burned, though not nearly as decomposed as you'd think it would be out here in the elements."

Bender nodded and began moving with Hanson toward the excavation. "It's the desert climate. Some of the most amazingly well-preserved mummies ever found turn up every once in a while out here in cactus country. Might make my job easier."

"Let's hope so," Hanson said. Murders used to be as rare as frog-hair in Roswell. This was the first apparent homicide to come up since he'd replaced Jim Valenti as Roswell's sheriff, and he knew the way he handled things today could make or break his reputation—a reputation he felt had already become somewhat tarnished a month back.

That was when he had summoned the state police and an army of sharpshooters to Brody Davis's UFO Center in response to an apparent hostage situation that had turned out to be nothing more than a series of unlikely communication foul-ups and misunderstandings, both on his part and on the part of Jim Valenti. People were going to be concerned when they learned about this corpse; if this really turned out to be a genuine, honest-to-God murder, Hanson knew he had to allay everyone's fears.

And find the killer.

The two men made small talk until they reached the site where the deputies had exhumed the body. Hanson saw that the remains had already been placed on a tarpaulin. Bender exchanged pleasant greetings with the others there, saving a big smile for Dina, whom he had dated a few times. Hanson held a hand up to his nose to block the faint spoiled-pot-roast smell rising from the corpse as the sun baked it. He began taking shallow breaths through his mouth.

Could be a lot worse, Hanson told himself, willing his stomach to lie still. *We could have fished this one out of a river, all rotten like in* Silence of the Lambs.

Bender donned his glasses and surgical gloves, then crouched beside the corpse, poking and prodding at the body and its charred clothing with one hand and a long, stainless-steel needle of some sort. It reminded Hanson of the blackboard pointers his teachers had used.

"From the condition of the clothes, I'd say the subject

has definitely been out here for a while," Bender said, speaking into his handheld Dictaphone for the official record. He wasn't blocking his nose, even though the stench was bad. Hanson realized that the pathologist must have seen and smelled a lot worse during his time.

Bender continued making his observations, using the efficient cadences of a seasoned county coroner. "I'd estimate the body may have been here for as long as a year, though lab tests will have to be done to confirm that. The subject is definitely a male, probably in his late forties or early fifties. The remains are badly burned, though it isn't apparent as yet whether those injuries were made prior to death or postmortem."

Bender examined the dead man's hands. "I find no rings or watches on the body. The subject either wasn't married or was robbed prior to his death." He prodded the corpse a bit more, then shut off the Dictaphone, muttering under his breath.

He looked up at Hanson. "Sorry, Randy. Can't tell you much more until I can get him onto the slab."

Bender stood up and stripped off his rubber gloves with a loud snap. He deposited them into a Baggie marked BIOHAZARD, then wiped his sweaty hands on his pants and approached Hanson. Behind the doctor, the two deputies were closing up the tarpaulin carefully, and preparing to move it into a nearby body bag and onto a stretcher. Heikenberry snapped a few more photos as the other deputies worked, then moved over to the excavation site.

"Hell of a thing, Randy," Bender said. "Seems like all we've been doing lately is digging up bodies around these parts. First that one that the congresswoman got involved with, then that girl who got buried alive out in Frazier Woods, and now this one. What's *with* folks these days?"

Hanson had found himself wondering the same thing quite often lately. "I dunno, Bill," he said as they began walking in the direction of their respective vehicles. "I've been doing law enforcement work for, what, eight years now? Seems like the last two years have had more excitement than the previous six put together."

Bender punched him playfully on the shoulder. "Well, you're the sheriff now, boy! Ain't it about time you took control of things, instead of lettin' the things control you?" The coroner was almost twice Hanson's age, but he always displayed a grandfatherly attitude toward him.

"That I will, Bill," Hanson said with a grin. As Bender continued toward his Jeep, Hanson turned back to look at his men. *My men. And they've been my men ever since Sheriff Valenti got fired.* Some days the fact that he was wearing the top cop badge seemed unreal to him, especially when he was still working out of the same offices where he had served as Valenti's senior deputy. Every day Hanson seemed to have to remind himself that he *deserved* to be in charge. After all, Valenti had screwed up several times, including his harassment of that geologist Grant Sorenson. Luckily for Valenti and the sheriff's department, Sorenson had never pressed charges; in fact, no one had heard from him in ages. He seemed to have simply disappeared. . . .

A chill ran down Hanson's spine, even though the sun was getting ever hotter and higher in the sky. He didn't want to think what he was thinking, and yet he had to consider the possibility: *Could this be Grant Sorenson's body?*

But Bender had said it had been out here for a year, which made it seem unlikely. And Sorenson was somewhat younger than Bender's age estimate. Still, the decomposition of the body—or lack thereof—might mean that it had been lying out here for a shorter period of time. Maybe the rotted clothes had just thrown Bender's estimate off. *We'll know soon enough,* Hanson thought, *once Bender does his lab tests.*

Hanson didn't like to even consider pointing the finger of suspicion toward Valenti. Jim had always treated him fairly, and had taught him a lot about the law enforcement profession. But Jim had been getting himself into some mighty strange situations during the last year, many of them involving teenage kids like that troublemaker Michael Guerin. And Valenti's involvement with the rescue of that girl—Laurie Dupree, he recalled—from her underground coffin out in the woods . . . that was suspicious as well. It had contributed to Valenti's firing, and to Hanson's own promotion.

But even out of the law enforcement loop, Valenti had *still* managed to get himself into some bizarre scrapes. The nonhostage situation at the UFO Center was one of them, as was the suicide of Alex Whitman a few months back. Hanson knew that most of the teens involved in these incidents were friends of Kyle Valenti, and that Jim had dated Amy DeLuca, the single mother of one of the kids, so it was no surprise that Valenti would cross paths with a lot of the same people repeatedly.

Still, some gut level instinct told Hanson that Jim was involved with the teens on some deeper level. And that his former boss was even now keeping some very significant secrets.

* * *

Jim Valenti had just taken a bite of the steaming hot chicken pot pie when the phone rang. He had microwaved it too long, and it burned his mouth as he grabbed the receiver. "Mussht a minnut," he mouthed into the phone, then spit the bite out into the kitchen sink. He flicked the water on and stooped to take a quick swig. *Better.*

He returned the phone to his ear. "Sorry about that. Hello?" He heard a familiar voice and grinned. "Oh, hi, Nicole. Yeah, I'm okay. I just took a bite of something too hot. What's up?"

As he listened to her, his eyes flickered over to the wall-mounted coatrack behind the door, where he used to keep his sheriff's jacket and hat. They had been replaced by a well-worn jeans jacket, a gray sweatshirt, and a couple of baseball caps.

"Sure, I can come in. Give me half an hour and I'll be there." He hung up the phone and stood for a moment, his hand still on the receiver.

Hanson wants me to come in to help ID a corpse they just dug up in the desert. Jim knew that at least Nicole thought it was a routine consultation, probably a way to check his mental missing persons files against whatever was in the department's computers. But he could feel in his bones that there was nothing about this call that would be routine.

Valenti already had some suspicions as to what or who might have caused the death. *Nasedo.* He knew that the alien had been pretty quick on the draw with his death-touch. He'd spent too many years chasing Nasedo's calling card, the swift-fading silver handprint that the shape-shifter left on his victims' bodies. Too long looking for proof that Valenti and his father had not been searching in vain to verify the existence of the aliens who moved freely among humans.

And he *had* been vindicated, as had his father. Not only did Valenti know that aliens had come to Roswell in the past, he also knew who and where they were in the present. He had even become their protector, a role with which he had grown comfortable, but which ultimately had cost him his job.

Nasedo had left more than a few corpses in his wake during the time when Max was taken by the military for study; could the body in the desert be just another nameless "man in black" that Nasedo had erased from existence?

Ignoring the pot pie now cooling on the kitchen counter, Valenti grabbed the phone and dialed a number that he had committed to memory. It rang three times, then a voice mail message came on.

"Max, this is Valenti. I'm headed in to the sheriff's office to consult on a case. They just found a body buried in the desert, and I have a feeling that Nasedo may have been involved somehow. I just wanted to give you the heads-up in case . . . well, you'll know if anything happens."

He hung up the phone. *Not the most articulate of phone messages, but it'll have to do. After all, it's not as though I have any conclusive evidence right now. But it's always best to be prepared.*

As he stepped toward the door, Jim Valenti decided that he did know one thing for certain: Whenever a dead body was unearthed in Roswell, trouble always was soon to follow.

The only question that remained was whether it would be human trouble or alien trouble.

5

Isabel Evans was bored. Not that she had expected today to be more exciting than any other day she'd spent helping out at her father's law office. But she found herself wishing desperately that something would happen to break up the repetition of photocopying and filing. *Anything at all.*

Mikio, her father's regular secretary, was out sick, and probably wouldn't be back for the rest of the week. Isabel suspected that morning sickness was what was keeping her home; the frail woman hadn't mentioned it, but Isabel knew that she and her husband had been trying to have a baby for months now. Isabel had thought of dreamwalking Mikio one evening to find out for sure, but she had never used her powers on a pregnant woman before, and she wasn't sure what the result would be. Besides, using her powers to eavesdrop on other people's thoughts and dreams merely to satisfy her own personal curiosity seemed sort of . . . rude. *Better not to take the risk.*

The phone hadn't rung for hours, and there weren't any appointments on the schedule until later in the afternoon, and she suspected that one "appointment" was actually a game of golf. But she wasn't about to press her father on his secrets. After all, she didn't want him doing the same to her.

"Isabel!" her father's voice shook her out of her bored trance-state, and she turned toward him with a start. "Didn't you hear me?"

"What? No, Daddy. I was—I guess I was spacing out." She smiled innocently, brushing a lock of her hair back off her face.

Phillip Evans rolled his eyes, then looked back at her with an understanding grin. "I need the Zurpat files, and Mrs. Tarrabon's phone number. It's under the 'R' heading for 'Raleigh.' That's her soon-to-be ex-husband."

Isabel sighed and swiveled in her chair, reaching for the computer mouse and keyboard. "If you know right where it is, why do you need me to get it for you?" she asked, her voice taking on a tone that her father sometimes unfairly described as "whiny."

"Honestly, Isabel. Do you think I should just pay you to sit here and doodle?" Her father stepped over next to the desk, pointing at a yellow legal pad that sat on top of it. Isabel glanced at it quickly, then blanched. She could almost feel the blood running out of her face. She *had* been doodling, lost in thought.

The designs she had sketched on the legal pad were alien symbols, pieces of the otherworldly cryptography she had seen in her dreams, in the desert, in the Granilith, and in the alien instruction book that Tess had forced Alex Whitman to translate for her last year.

Though the moment passed almost instantly, apprehension flooded Isabel as if she had been standing there, gape-jawed, for hours. What if her father questioned her about the symbols? What if he found out she was an alien? Would she betray her brother and Michael? Would she be put into a white room the way Max had been, examined, prodded, maybe even dissected—

She forced her mind to snap back from its building chain-reaction of fear. Offering her father a wan smile, she said, "No, Daddy. Of course not. I'm just feeling a little cranky today."

Then her father did the unthinkable. Sitting on the edge of the desk, he grabbed the legal tablet. Squinting slightly, he pored over her drawings "These are . . . what *are* these?"

Isabel shifted uncomfortably in her chair, though she hoped he wouldn't notice. "Oh, you know. Just some stuff I saw on the cover of this new rock band's CD." She forced herself to maintain a pleasant expression.

"Mmmmm," Phillip said, nodding his head. One hand went up and scratched at his graying temples momentarily. "For a moment, I thought maybe you were working on some kind of art project. Like something for college or . . ." He let that thought trail off, but quickly moved on to a new one. "Speaking of which, what's going on with your college plans? Did you ever make a decision about Santa Fe State?"

She winced inwardly. *Out of the frying pan and into the fire.* Her father wasn't concentrating on her alien doodles any longer, but he had sidestepped into another subject that was very nearly as touchy. A few months ago, Isabel had been ready to leave Roswell. She had been accepted into a college in San Francisco, had planned to leave in

June—she was even looking at dormitory brochures—when Alex Whitman had died. And then Max had stepped on her future, *hard,* imposing his will as King Zan, the ruler of their alien homeworld of Antar.

She remembered what her brother had said like it was yesterday. "Isabel, if I have to, I will do everything in my power to keep you here. I will tell our parents you have a drug problem. I will notify your teachers that you have cheated on every test for the last three years. If you ever leave Roswell without my consent, I will physically drag you back. For the last time, the answer is 'no.' Period."

And with that, her future had crumbled. Coming directly after Alex's death, Max's threats were the blow that had blown apart the fragile house of cards that her life had become. Her *human* life. She liked to believe she *was* human. Not Vilandra, the alien princess who had betrayed her royal family.

In the months that followed, even Isabel herself had noticed that she was becoming more moody than was normal for her; she knew she hadn't fully forgiven Max, even though she had told him that she had. On top of it all, lately she had been receiving unsettling visitations from Alex's ghost; she didn't know if she was experiencing an actual haunting, or some psychological manifestation of the responsibility she felt for Alex's death, even though it had been caused by Tess. But she found that the spectral talks had an up side: They seemed to help her work through moments of crisis.

Of course, Alex's ghost was nowhere to be found during *this* moment of crisis. Isabel squirmed again, and offered her father another too-perky smile. "I don't think Santa Fe

State is for me, Daddy. I think I'm going to enroll in Eastern New Mexico University here in town."

"But that's only a two-year college," Phillip said, an edge of concern in his voice.

"I know, but if I want to, I can easily transfer to the parent college in Portales to complete my four-year degree." She leaned forward, putting her hand on top of his. She grabbed the legal pad with the other. "Don't worry," she said. "I'm not going to live with you and Mom forever. I'm going to have my own life soon enough."

Phillip patted her hand and stood up. She could sense the relief he felt and knew that she'd chosen the right answer. "All right, honey. It's not that we want you out of the house, it's just that we want to be sure you make the best decisions about what to do with your life." He moved back toward his office door, then turned to face her again. "I'll still need those files, though. *And* Mrs. Tarrabon's phone number."

She gave him a mock-military salute. "Yes, sir. Coming right up." As soon as he entered the office, she wiped her hand across the top of the legal pad, her alien powers breaking down the molecular structure of the ink and even smoothing out the indentations left by her pen. Within moments, the pad was clean, as if she had never drawn on the top sheet at all. She set it down on the edge of the desk and turned back to the computer.

A minute later, she had found the phone number her father needed, printed it out, then crossed over to the file cabinets to pull the hard copy of the Zurpat files. As she grabbed them, she heard a faint sound behind her, causing the fine hairs on the back of her neck to stand up. She turned, her body tense. But her anxiety quickly drained away when she saw who had entered the room.

"Jesse!" The cute young lawyer, Jesse Ramirez, had recently begun working at her father's firm. He smiled at her, his teeth gleaming white. Gesturing toward the lone iris in the vase he had just placed on her desk, he said, "Hi, Isabel. I brought you a little something."

"It's beautiful!" She grinned, but restrained herself from hugging him. Not with her father in the office. "I love irises."

"Well, I thought a rose might be a bit much." He gestured toward the door to her father's office. "Is my boss in?"

"He is indeed," Isabel said, nodding pertly. Hugging the files to her chest, she stepped around her desk, making sure to brush her arm ever so slightly across Jesse's chest as she headed to Dad's office. Noticing that he hesitated a bit, blushing red up to his ears, she barely restrained herself from grinning.

"Daddy, Mr. Ramirez is back from his deposition," she said after stepping into her father's office, with Jesse following behind her. "And here are your files."

Phillip looked up from the paperwork strewn across his desk and took the files that Isabel offered him. "Jesse, how did it go this morning? You look a bit . . . out of breath."

Jesse shot Isabel a quick look as she walked back to the door. She had to bite her tongue to keep from laughing.

"It's, um, pretty hot out today," Jesse said.

She sat back down behind her desk and picked up the iris, sniffing it. The scent was subtle, but she loved the blend of colors in the flower. It was sweet of Jesse to bring it to her.

She was really beginning to like him. He'd come to town to visit his mother after his graduation from Harvard Law School, and then had decided to stay. Her father had snapped him up quickly, and Isabel had been just as quick on the uptake. She had met him on July 5—his birthday, coincidentally—during the 54th Annual Roswell UFO Festival.

They'd only had a few real dates so far—all kept discreetly concealed from her parents, of course—but Isabel already sensed a real chemistry developing between them. She loved his sly, almost deadpan sense of humor, and how he always treated her with respect. At times it almost felt like an old 1950s TV courtship; he hadn't done anything to rush their relationship, allowing it to blossom and grow on its own.

Jesse Ramirez is a keeper. She wasn't certain she'd be the one keeping him, or if they would eventually drift apart, but she knew he was special. Like Alex had been. She hadn't given Alex enough of a chance when he was alive, thinking of him as too young, too awkward, unworthy of her. She knew now that her attitude toward him had been unfair snobbery. As the alien part of her life came more and more into the forefront, she felt that the snooty, immature aspects of her personality had begun retreating. Alex had patiently pursued her, undaunted by the initially chilly reception she had given him.

Most importantly, Alex had never treated her any differently because of his knowledge of her alien origins. His attraction toward her had never been swayed by the countless light-years that separated their respective genetic codes.

Isabel looked over at the yellow legal pad, its molecules

so recently scrambled by her alien powers. Biting her lip, she glanced toward the office door. *What would happen if I told Jesse the truth? Would he accept me, or would he run away in fear?*

As long as she didn't know the answer to those questions, Isabel was afraid she might not be able to let him get too close.

6

Max resisted the urge to go back into the Crashdown. He had already been there twice today; first, to see Liz earlier this morning, then just a short time ago to let the others in on his plan. Michael had been antsy about the possibility that the diaries might get lost, but Max assured him they were as safe as anything else in the apartment, and possibly safer.

Ever since Tess had retrieved the Granilith's instruction book from inside the library wall, Max had been experimenting with his powers, trying to do something similar. The closest he had come so far was to use his molecular powers to open a hole inside a wall that was already hollow, place something inside the hollow area, and then restore the wall's molecular structure to its original form. Though he hadn't yet perfected the trick, he was already confident he could use it to hide important items without detection. Max thought that Michael's only worry should be whether there were mice living in his apartment walls that might blunder into harm's way.

Leaning against the street-side wall of the UFO Center, Max sipped his cherry cola and winced. He wished he had remembered to add some Tabasco sauce to it before he left, to cut the sickly sweet flavor with something pungently spicy. For some reason, the taste wasn't quite the same if he used his powers to change it; better to do it the old-fashioned way.

A woman walked by, her toddler following after her on a harness-leash device. The little boy held a bendable green alien figure in his hand and waved it happily at Max. The real alien smiled and waved back, then looked down the street. *Kyle's late. At this rate, I'm not going to have enough time to pull this off.*

But a moment later Max saw Kyle Valenti crossing the street, half trotting as he looked first in one direction, then the other. Max didn't consider Kyle a terribly close friend, but they had certainly come a long way in their relationship over the past two years. Max had stolen Liz away from Kyle, but had later saved Kyle's life after he'd been shot during a gunfight between Sheriff Valenti and FBI Agent Daniel Pierce. Along the way, there had been a lot of twists and turns, and Max knew that Kyle still had feelings for Liz. Still, like his father, Kyle was dependable in the extreme. If not always precisely on time.

"It's about time you got here, Kyle," Max said, realizing belatedly that his annoyance was a little too evident in his tone.

Kyle's eyebrows knit together in puzzlement, and he scowled. "Hello to you, too, Max. I guess if you need someone else to act as your human patsy, you can always invite somebody new into your 'I Know an Alien' club."

Max held up his hands in a gesture of peace. "Sorry, Kyle. I'm glad you're here, and I appreciate your help. But we're really going to have to hurry now."

Kyle nodded. "So what do you need me to do?"

Max handed him the cell phone he had borrowed from Liz. "I already made sure that Brody was gone from the Center. I have to get into some of his private files without his finding out about it, but he could come back any minute. I need you to stand lookout. If you see Brody coming, just hit the call button and I'll get out of there."

"Uh, hello? There's only *one* exit from the Center. Don't you think he'll see you?"

"Not if you distract him properly. Or spot him well before he gets here." Max clicked his own cell phone on and noticed that the message icon was flashing. *No time to listen to it now. I'll check it later,* he thought. He glanced at his Chevy, which was parked on the UFO Center's side of the street. Everything was ready. Then he moved toward the door of the Center.

"Okay, I'll do my best." Kyle leaned back against the car and began scanning up and down the street as small groups of passersby went about their business.

The air around Max's hand glowed slightly as he held it over the lock at the UFO Center door. Momentarily, a slight click told him the lock had opened, and he ducked inside the museum.

He moved carefully down the steps in the dim greenish light of the museum displays. The Center was actually converted from an old fallout shelter, so absolutely no natural light came into the place. Thankfully, the air was only slightly stale, since oxygen pumps ventilated the building.

Having worked there part-time for the last two years, Max knew the layout of the Center quite well. He remembered the first time he had walked into the place. It was shortly after he had revealed his secret to Liz, and he had been at the Crashdown with her. A woman had forgotten her change, and he'd followed her to the museum to return it. Milton Ross, who'd operated the Center in those days, had offered him a job, convinced that he, too, was a "true believer" in the existence of aliens.

Max grinned, thinking of Milton, who had always wanted to meet an alien face to face, little realizing that he'd actually had a *bona fide* extraterrestrial working for him. Milton was the one who had come up with most of the cheesy displays and props featured in the museum's exhibits, and even though he had sometimes privately acknowledged that many of the displays existed purely for the entertainment of the audience, publicly he took his alien lore extremely seriously. And he had expected Max to be just as serious when giving tours of the facility. Still, Max often had trouble pointing to some of the little green men that festooned the place without cracking a joke.

As Max made his way past one of the glass cases, the dark ovoid eyes of one of the little green men caught his attention. He turned and studied it for a second. Its hand was raised, spindly fingers splayed imploringly, as though suing for peace. But Max understood well enough that this wasn't a completely accurate portrait. Although the ship that had brought him and the others here in their gestation pods had been on an ostensibly peaceful mission, the aliens who had abducted Charles Dupree, and probably others, for their genetic codes had a thing or two to learn about politeness and civility.

Not to mention the fact that the shape-shifting Nasedo, one of two survivors from the pod-ship and protector to Max and the other half-aliens, had committed more than his share of killings over the years. And who knew what the other surviving alien had done? Was he or she *also* killing to survive, just as Nasedo had?

Max also knew that the aliens from his homeworld didn't need to be physically present to affect the lives of humans on Earth. Brody Davis had bought the UFO Center from Milton last year, partly to continue Milton's research into abductions. And although he couldn't prove it, Max suspected that Milton had sold the Center to Brody while under some kind of mind control; Max knew for certain that Brody's body was sometimes hijacked telepathically by Larek, one of the politicians in the planetary system that contained Max's homeworld.

As he made his way to the locked file-storage area, Max pondered the quandary he was in. *Do I even know of a single instance of positive alien interaction with humans?* Of course he did; he, Isabel, and Michael had done many positive things. *But would those good deeds have needed doing if we hadn't been here, disrupting people's lives in Roswell in the first place?* Kyle wouldn't have been shot, Laurie Dupree wouldn't have been kidnapped, Alex wouldn't be dead, and all the crises their friends and companions had been put through wouldn't have happened.

And yet, Liz would have died if I hadn't healed her. Brody's daughter, and the other children Max had healed last Christmas, would still be sick as well; some of them might even be dead by now. Max shook his head as if to scatter his doubts, though he knew they would return. He knew that he brooded far too often about such things—the others even teased him about it sometimes—but understanding the behavior and changing it were two different things.

Max reached forward and put his hand up to the key pad that Brody had installed by the door that led into the locked storage room. Brody didn't much trust padlocks, but the electronic lock was no less simple for Max to bypass, requiring only a slight nudge from his alien powers.

Inside the chamber, he flicked on the light switch and took a breath of the dank, musty air. At least it didn't smell of mold or mildew; by the time he'd sold the Center, Milton had finished moving everything onto storage racks and had filed all the paperwork in archive boxes. But unlike Milton, Brody was less open about allowing Max access to the storage area. Max hadn't really questioned him as to why. Perhaps he was hiding something private having to do with his own abductions and encounters with aliens. Or maybe he was reticent for reasons entirely unrelated to aliens.

Max decided he didn't have time to concern himself with that for now. Rounding the corner of one set of racks, he found the older boxes stacked up near the back wall. Some hadn't been touched in years, while others appeared to have been explored far more recently. Unsurprisingly, several dozen of the file boxes were marked 1947. Because these were such banner years in alien-abduction lore, Max expected the records from that time to be fairly extensive.

Max began to pull boxes out, flipping the lids up and reading the titles of the files inside. There were several boxes of books, and many more boxes of period newspapers and magazines. In a surprisingly short time, he hit paydirt: files on people in the area who claimed to have been abducted.

He scanned the names for clues. Belmont, Cash, Crouch, Davis, Denham, Dutch, Ellington, Forrester, Gaines . . . there were probably over a hundred files in the box. None of them were the name DuPree, he noted. He pulled the "Crouch" file and opened it. Inside was a clipping from the newspaper, indicating that Jim's father and Kyle's grandfather, Sheriff James Valenti, Sr., had found a woman wandering in the desert—Darlene Crouch—who'd had no idea how she had gotten there from her car in Tucson. Crouch didn't look like Isabel or Tess, but Max couldn't rule her out either. *Just because Michael looks exactly like Charles Dupree, we can't necessarily assume that the rest of us will resemble our own human genetic templates.*

Max pulled another file and skimmed it until he was reasonably certain that Mrs. Denham wasn't one of their gene donors. She was Japanese, the wife of an American soldier stationed at the military base.

He put that file aside and had reached for another when his cell phone rang. The sound startled him; he had tuned out everything but his purpose here, and he dropped the folder. Bending to get it, he toggled his phone on. "Max here."

Kyle's voice was tinny through the small receiver. "Brody just drove by, looking for a parking space. You'd better get out of there."

"Got it. Stall him if you can."

"I'll try. Damn! Someone pulled out up the block. He'll be parked soon enough."

"I'm leaving now," Max said, then switched the phone off. Scanning quickly, he saw some empty boxes piled in the corner, apparently left over from when everything had been transferred to the archival boxes. He grabbed three and dumped the contents of one of the 1947 abductee boxes into one of them. Replacing the now-empty archive box on the shelf, he dropped the Denham file into it, then put the lid on top.

Max scowled for a moment, realizing that the box looked out of place now. He ran his hand over the top of it and others beside it, drawing dust from the others and evenly distributing it across all of them. Satisfied that the archive box now looked relatively undisturbed, Max lifted the trio of boxes and headed toward the door.

He switched off the light and closed the door, the click of the electronic lock behind him a reassuring sound. As quickly as he could, he made his way through the exhibits and back up the steps. Once he had reached the door, he cracked it an inch. Sunlight streamed in, blinding him momentarily.

Outside, he could see a nervous Kyle approaching Brody, who was walking toward the Center, carrying a bag. Max balanced the boxes against the doorjamb with his leg and stretched his hand out, pointing at the parking meter that Brody was just about to pass.

Max knew that he didn't need his hands to use his powers, but they certainly helped him focus his concentration. He squinted, feeling the power surging from his mind down to his arm, then coursing into his hand. There was a slight, almost imperceptible electrical crackle around his hand as the power built up. Abruptly, Max released it.

Right next to Brody, one of the parking meters suddenly exploded open, the metal change door striking the sidewalk with a clatter. Brody jumped to the side, startled, almost dropping his bag, as quarters, dimes, and nickels cascaded down onto the sidewalk. The jingle sounded like a slot machine paying out at Vegas.

"What happened?" Kyle said to Brody as he neared him. Brody was staring at the parking meter in surprise as coins continued spilling out.

"I don't know," Brody said in his slight English accent. "It just *exploded*!"

"Well, we can't just leave it like this," Kyle said. He gestured toward Brody. "Can we use your bag to clean all this up?" He crouched by the pile of metal and money spilled all over the sidewalk.

"Uh, I guess," Brody responded. He removed a box— some new computer component, from what Max could see—from the bag and set it on the sidewalk, crouching next to Kyle.

The moment Brody began to pick up the change, Max darted out from inside the UFO Center, moving quickly toward his car. He put the box with the files behind the driver's seat, and put one of the two empty ones on top of it.

Checking to make sure that Brody's attention was still occupied, Max moved back to the Center's door, still carrying one empty box. He opened the door and put a foot inside, then called out to Brody and Kyle.

"Kyle! Brody! What's up? You guys need any help?"

Brody looked up in surprise. "Max, what are you doing here? I gave you the day off."

Max moved toward them, gesturing with the box. "I needed some empty boxes to move some stuff. We had a bunch at the Center, and I didn't think you'd mind me borrowing some."

"No . . . of course not," Brody said, puzzlement still etched onto his face.

"What happened?" Max was near them now, and he bent to look at the parking meter. *Not a bad monkey-wrenching job,* he thought.

"It just exploded," Kyle said, still picking up coins. Must be faulty or something."

"If you've got your cell phone, why don't you call the city services number and report this?" Brody asked.

Now it was Max's turn to look quizzical. "I've got my phone, but not the city number."

"Just call police nonemergency," Kyle offered. "It's 555-6770."

"Call it often?" Brody asked with a smirk.

"My dad *did* used to be the sheriff. They *do* kind of work with the police, you know."

As Kyle and Brody finished picking up the change, Max called the number Kyle had given him and reported the broken meter. By the time he had finished, Brody and Kyle were also done, both of them poking at the wreckage of the meter with strange looks on their faces.

"They'll be by soon. I told them to come pick up the money from you at the museum," Max said, looking at Brody. "I've got some plans, but if you need me to stick around, I can . . ." He trailed off.

Brody waved him off with a bit of a tired smile. "No, go on. Just get the door for me, now that I've got a new scanner *and* a bag of loose change to carry."

Max opened the door for Brody, then said, "Thanks for the boxes. I'll bring them back on my next shift."

"No hurry," Brody called out as he went down the stairs.

Max got into his car while Kyle hopped into the passenger's side.

"Did you get what you needed?" Kyle asked.

"I hope so. At least it's a damn good lead," Max said.

As they pulled out of the parking spot, Kyle pointed over at the broken meter. "Your work, I assume?"

"Yeah," Max said, feeling a bit embarrassed.

"What, you didn't think I could distract him?" Kyle shook his head, grinning. "Man, you aliens sure are a distrustful bunch."

7

Jim Valenti pulled into the parking lot of the Sheriff's station on East Fifth Street. He had done it thousands of times before, but this time he had to mentally force himself not to park in the employees' section. Each time he had come here recently had felt like a kick in the belly. Law enforcement had been in his blood since he was a child, and had stayed with him even after his father had been disgraced and removed from duty.

Like father, like son, he thought ruefully. Both of them had become embroiled in the world of aliens, which had cost them their livelihoods. Valenti sat back in his seat, closing his eyes, the past replaying like a movie in his mind.

His father, James, Sr., had been a deputy when the alien ship had crashed at Pohlman Ranch in the summer of 1947. The resulting cover-up had sparked his interest in UFOs and alien visitations, and he avidly worked cases of unexplained disappearances and reported abductions in the area of Chaves County and beyond.

In 1955, James got a copy of the book *Among Us,* written by noted UFO author William Atherton, and read and reread his copy of it so many times that the bindings had broken. Atherton was clear in his text that he felt aliens were already on Earth, walking among humans unnoticed. He knew the truth, but that knowledge would cost him. Four years after his book was published, Atherton disappeared; UFO devotees remained convinced that he had been abducted by aliens, who sought to punish him for revealing the truth about their existence.

In November 1959, James Valenti, Sr., worked on a murder case that would forever alter the trajectory of his life, and that of his eight-year-old son, Jim, Jr. The body of a man was found in the desert, his flesh cooked from within. James had arrived at the site just before dusk, and he and others were startled to find that as the evening sky grew darker, a glowing silver handprint had become visible on the victim's chest.

No other clues to the identity of the man's killer were ever found, and the murder remained unsolved to this day. But the elder James Valenti never forgot it. Nor did he stop looking for signs of aliens, even when it weakened his credibility as the town's sheriff. His enthusiasm rubbed off on his son; many times they would take fishing trips or go camping not for the recreational experience, but rather for the chance to explore the lands around Roswell and the skies above it, searching for evidence of otherworldly visitations. Young Jim became intimately familiar with the Eagle Rock Military Base outside of town, looking in from the perimeter fence. He wouldn't actually enter the base until years later.

Jim had just turned twenty-two when his family's world came crashing down around him. First, his mother developed inoperable breast cancer, but it metastasized so quickly that there was little the doctors could do to stop its spread. Constantly in pain, she'd died in her sleep in the summer of 1970. Jim always suspected that she may have hastened her own death by taking multiple painkillers, but he had never discussed the matter with his father.

A few months later, the body of a young woman named Sheila Hubble had been found in a condition similar to that of the 1959 corpse, right down to the presence of the silver handprint. She had been killed in the rest room area at the side of Pepper's Café, near her car. All signs pointed to a stranger who had surprised her, rather than an attack by someone she knew. Her husband, Everett Hubble, had seen a man running away from the car, and while the official police reports chalked the incident up to a failed car theft, Hubble had believed differently.

Everett Hubble was a veteran of the Vietnam War, and a man dangerously on the edge. Like Atherton, Hubble believed that aliens walked among us. After his wife's murder, Hubble became a man driven by vengeance, determined to track down Sheila's killer, whom he believed to be a shape-shifting alien.

Late in 1972, Everett Hubble returned to Roswell, supposedly on the trail of the alien who had killed his wife. Hubble and Sheriff Valenti tracked the man to a silo outside of town, and in the ensuing confrontation, Hubble shot the drifter dead. James took the fall for the shooting, but when it turned out that the drifter was fully human—

and not one of the aliens whom Hubble had hunted—the sheriff was stripped of his job. Recently, Jim had come across the newspaper headline from that fateful day, December 8, 1972: "Roswell Sheriff Taken In for Questioning for the Silo Murder."

The toll of that year's events had weighed hard on Jim's father, and he sank further and further into depression, alcohol, and insane-sounding ravings about aliens. On Halloween night in 1973, events came to a head when James, Sr., took two teenage pranksters hostage, claiming they were aliens. The boys had come in costume to throw toilet paper into the neighborhood trees, little realizing the danger awaiting them from the grief-crazed ex-sheriff.

In the ensuing scandal, Jim had had little choice but to commit his father to a mental institution. At first he'd visited daily, then weekly, then once or twice a month. Over the years the gaps had grown in length, even as his father's lucidity progressively dwindled. When Jim married Michelle Greene, James, Sr., had been released to attend the wedding but had been removed before the ceremony even started because of his loud, incoherent rantings. Only when he promised not to speak did the attending nurse allow him to witness his own son's nuptials.

James, Sr., rarely spoke at all after that. He smiled and played a bit with young Kyle, on the infrequent occasions when Jim had brought his son to visit. But for the most part the old man seemed distracted, even as the toddler climbed all over him as though he were a jungle gym. Once, after Kyle had offended his grandfather with some innocent, childish comment, James had yelled at the little boy so harshly that his grandson had begged to stay home the next time Jim visited the hospital. And the time after that.

Eventually, Jim began staying home as well. He became a deputy under his father's successor, then eventually became sheriff himself. His marriage to Michelle didn't last, but Jim kept custody of Kyle. Although the two of them were quite close, Jim didn't share much of his continuing interest in UFOs with his son. *Better to let the boy discover his own path*, he had thought at the time, *and break this endless cycle of searching for things that aren't there*.

And then, almost two years ago, Jim's life had taken another detour, this time straight into the twilight zone. A man had fired a gun inside the Crashdown Café, striking young waitress Liz Parker in the belly. Or so some eyewitnesses had claimed. They'd also sworn that Max Evans had put his hand over the wound, and that Liz had gotten up shortly thereafter, apparently unharmed. The only trace of the gunshot was some powder residue soaked in ketchup, a splatter of blood on her dress—and a glowing silver handprint on Liz's abdomen.

Valenti's investigation into the shooting led him to begin surveillance on Max Evans, and eventually his sister Isabel as well, along with Max's closest friend, Michael Guerin. All of the threads of Valenti's past began to converge then, leading him to visit William Atherton's old home, a geodesic dome in Marathon, Texas. There, he was knocked unconscious by FBI Agent Kathleen Topolsky, who was also spying on Max and the others. Jim soon discovered that Atherton was the man who had been burned to a crisp in 1959.

Later, Everett Hubble returned to town and abducted

Max Evans, accusing the teen of being the shape-shifting killer of Sheila Hubble. The sheriff was forced to shoot Hubble in order to protect Max, and in doing so came to understand that his obsessions were turning him into a man every bit as dangerous as Hubble had been—and just as "out there" as his father had become prior to his unraveling. Jim reconnected with his father at the time of that incident, and both men remained on the path toward healing today.

Shortly after saving Max from Hubble, Valenti had learned the whole truth. Aliens *did* walk among humans, and Max, Isabel, and Michael were three of them. Aware that government forces were suspicious of an alien presence in Roswell, Valenti began to act as the teens' protector. In his eyes they were innocents, deserving of the same rights as any other law-abiding citizens. But because he shared their secret—and because their very existence validated virtually everything he and his father had ever believed about extraterrestrial life—Jim Valenti felt closer to the so-called "Pod Squad" than he cared to admit.

His allegiance had gotten him into trouble, both by causing him to bend rules on the job, and by straining his relationship with his own son. Kyle also learned of the alien presence—the hard way. During an altercation with a government operative at the UFO Center, Valenti accidentally shot Kyle, forcing Max to use his healing powers to save him. Now Jim was even more indebted to Max and the others, which had affected his professional and ethical decisions even as the web of alien conspiracy around Roswell continued to tighten.

Near the same time, the original guardian of the

aliens—a shape-changing man who was known only as Nasedo—came back to the town, bringing with him Tess Harding. She was another teenage alien, whom Nasedo had raised separately from the others. After Nasedo's death, Valenti had taken Tess into his own home, where she'd lived with him and Kyle until her recent departure from the planet.

But protecting the four alien teens had proved too hazardous for Valenti; earlier this year, he had been forced out of his job as sheriff, just like his father.

No, not like Dad. I was fired for protecting the innocent.

But in his heart, Jim knew the truth. He had transferred his obsession with UFOs over to the alien quartet. Even his relationship with Kyle was suffering because of his commitment to Max and his friends; how could he expect that his career wouldn't have suffered as well? The job hadn't prepared him for secret government agencies infiltrating the town, attacks by rival alien races, or threats from geologists trying to conquer the world at the behest of strange, blue, otherworldly crystals.

A sharp knock on his car window startled Valenti out of his reverie. His hand automatically went to the holster between the car's seats, but the weapon was no longer there. In the split second that this knowledge came, he looked to see who was standing outside his car.

He relaxed, relieved to see Deputy Owen Blackwood, one of his oldest friends in the department. The tall, dark-haired Mesaliko Indian grinned down at him, his thumbs hooked into his leather duty belt.

"You okay there, Jim?" Blackwood asked as Valenti rolled down the window.

"Yeah, thanks Owen," Jim responded. "I was just . . . reminiscing. Coming back here tends to do that to me." He unbuckled his seat belt and exited his vehicle.

"Yep," Blackwood said simply. The taciturn deputy held out his hand. Valenti shook it vigorously.

"So, you know why Hanson called me in?"

"We retrieved a body out near Tenpipe Bluff this morning. I think he wants to get your thoughts on it."

Jim nodded, shifting his jaw a bit so as not to clench his teeth. "Ah. Well, I've got nothing *better* to do with my life these days than help the sheriff's department out with their cases," he said, trying to keep the bitterness out of his voice.

Blackwood looked a bit uncomfortable. "You got a new job yet, Jim?"

Valenti looked away quickly. "No, not yet. It's . . . well, you know . . ."

"Yeah." Blackwood added, "Well, I'll keep my ears open for anything interesting." He cleared his throat, then offered, "Maggie and I want to have you and Kyle out for supper some night. You be up for that?"

"Sure, sure," Jim said, nodding. He gestured toward the station. "I'd better get in there. I'm sure Hanson's waiting."

"Good to see you again, Jim," Blackwood said, then shook his hand a final time and headed back toward his Jeep.

Valenti watched him go, wistfulness filling his heart. He looked back toward the station, willing his legs to start walking.

Gotta go in sometime. And it's not like I'm being charged with anything.

But hearing that a new corpse had been discovered in the desert made him shudder just a bit, even in the hot desert air.

Walking into the station's familiar, somewhat run-down confines—unarmed and wearing casual civilian clothes—made the former sheriff feel positively naked. Valenti nodded in greeting to Nicole Feldstein, who was seated behind the reception desk. She gave him a wave, but since she was on the phone, she just pointed him toward his old office.

Jim knocked on the doorjamb to Hanson's outer office. Valenti decided to play it dumb, not letting on what he knew until after he saw the cards Hanson played. "Knock, knock, Randy. You wanted to talk to me?"

Hanson stood up and moved around his desk toward Valenti, his body language clearly showing that he wasn't inviting his former boss in. "Jim, thanks for coming by. How are things going for you and Kyle?"

"They're *going*," Valenti said noncommittally. "What can I do for you?"

"Well, we've got a bit of a mystery on our hands with this body we found, and I think you might be able to help some. If you don't mind, of course."

"Not at all," Valenti said, a thin, humorless smile on his lips. "I've got a bit of free time today."

"Then let's go down to the dungeon," Hanson said, moving past Valenti and into the hall. Jim noticed that, unlike Blackwood, Hanson hadn't offered him a handshake.

They moved down a set of back stairs to the area that had been called "the dungeon" since before James Valenti,

Sr., became sheriff. It was a small morgue, equipped with just enough equipment to be functional when necessary. But since most of the autopsies in the area were done up in Albuquerque, the room was only rarely used.

The smell hit Valenti about halfway down. He recognized the stench of death, though this was more acrid than usual. When they entered the room, he saw why. Stretched out on the table was the thoroughly burned body of a man. Working over him was Bill Bender, who was muttering notes into a small Dictaphone as he prodded at different parts of the charred corpse.

Before Hanson could say anything, Bender looked up and grinned in Valenti's direction. "Jim. Good to see you."

Valenti grinned back. "Howdy, Bill. It's been a while."

Bender held up his gloved hands, palms out. "You'll excuse me not shaking your hand, Jim."

"Sure thing."

Hanson spoke up. "A couple of rabbit hunters found this body buried up on Tenpipe Bluff this morning. Look at all familiar?"

Jim studied what was left of the corpse's face for a moment, but felt no spark of recognition. Hanson gestured, and Bender pulled back the drape over the body's torso. Valenti sucked his breath in, his eyes widening with surprise. A deep impression of a human hand was seared deeply into the body's torso.

"Sorry, Randy. Can't say as I recognize the man."

"You *sure,* Jim? He's got a handprint burned right into his chest. Looks a lot like those photos you used to show us of people who were supposedly killed by aliens." Hanson stared at Valenti, watching him closely.

He's almost right about that, Valenti thought. Aloud, he said, "Not exactly, Randy. Those handprints were silver, and they glowed. Besides, they always faded away after a day or two."

Hanson's tone was snide. "Hmmm. Pretty convenient. So maybe our victim was done in by an Earthling after all."

My, he's actually starting to sound like the town sheriff. Valenti felt some mild surprise at how much the young sheriff's confidence had increased since the city-wide power failure a few months back. The chaos created by that incident must have shown Hanson just how unprepared for the job he had been back then.

Still, Valenti couldn't help but rise to his replacement's provocation, at least a little. "That's fine police work, Sheriff. Planet Earth is where I'd have started looking for suspects, too."

"Take another look at the man," Hanson said, eyes narrowing. "You sure you don't recognize him?"

Once again, Valenti studied the charred rictus that was the corpse's face, but still couldn't figure out who it might be. "Not much to go on here, Randy. The body's been burned beyond recognition. Did you find any clothes or personal effects with him?"

Bender gestured to a tattered and scorched pile of fabric over on the countertop. "That's all we've got. Seems to be what's left of a two-tone brown polo shirt, a white cotton tank top, and blue jeans. But there are some other identifying features." Using his fingers and a stainless-steel pointer, he displayed a small metal object that was lodged in the cooked flesh by the elbow joint. "He's got a pin in his elbow, probably put there because of a dislocation or a fracture. It appears to be about five years old."

Bender looked at Hanson, who gave him a slight nod; Valenti saw the wordless exchange out of the corner of his eye. *Something's wrong here. They're playing games with me.*

Valenti turned to the new sheriff. "Okay, Randy, I taught you most of what you know, so you can stop treating me like some freshwater hick. Who *is* this?"

Hanson stared at him for a moment, as if measuring him. Then, to Bender, he said, "Tell him."

"We matched this corpse up to some dental records, and Doc Wiesten confirmed that he inserted this after an altercation you and your men had with the decedent a few years back. Jim, this man is *Hank Whitmore.*"

Valenti's mind whirled. He remembered the fight Bender mentioned. Before Whitmore's third wife had left him, he had taken to beating on her pretty hard. The sheriff's deputies were called to the trailer park one night, where they interrupted a bloody fracas between Whitmore and his wife. Hank had resisted arrest so vehemently that they'd broken his arm just trying to cuff him. Valenti even remembered young Michael Guerin staring at him from behind the trailer's screen door. The boy, not quite a teenager back then, had seemed more relieved than frightened.

"Huh," Valenti said, at a loss. Whitmore had moved out of Roswell more than a year ago.

"Didn't you tell me you *saw* Whitmore last year, right before he left town?" He could tell that Hanson was finally getting to the point.

Valenti nodded. "Yeah. He came by the office upstairs. Told me he was going down to Las Cruces to take a job.

Said he was taking the trailer, and offered to sign anything I needed for his foster child's emancipation."

"Well, he never made it to Las Cruces, Jim. And he didn't take his trailer. The park finally sold it as abandoned a few months ago."

Valenti nodded. He felt a prickly sensation in his spine as he considered Hank Whitmore's likely fate. After all, Nasedo had killed many times before, always leaving a silver handprint behind as a calling card. Because Hank had been so abusive toward Michael, Nasedo could very well have considered him a mortal threat to the boy. Perhaps Nasedo had been especially angry when he had killed Whitmore, leaving the deep, hand-shaped wound on the corpse's chest. *And Nasedo was a shape-shifter. Maybe he came to my office posing as Whitmore as a way of covering his tracks. After all, who would go looking for the corpse of a man everybody believes is still alive?*

But Valenti knew that that explanation would never be believed, even if he *were* to reveal the truth of it.

"You know, I seem to recall that we held his foster son in the pokey upstairs for a while," Hanson said. "Back when we thought he might have had something to do with his foster father's disappearance. Michael Guerin was his name, right?"

"Yeah, that's him," said Valenti, nodding. "We did pick him up and question him about that. But then Whitmore came back and saw me in my office, and that was that. There wasn't any disappearance, so I had to turn the Guerin boy loose."

"Something else occurs to me, Jim. Last fall, we found that other body buried out in the desert, just like this one was. It was burned up, and those bones were fused together."

"Where are you going with this, Randy? The lab tests showed that those bones were over forty years old." Valenti's eyes narrowed. He was beginning to lose his patience.

"Yeah, that's what they showed all right. But remember that we found Michael Guerin's pocketknife near the burial site?"

"And he was cleared of any suspicion. Good grief, Randy, *I* was the one who told you why his knife was out there."

Hanson puffed up his chest, fixing Valenti with an even more critical stare. "Yep, I remember that. *You* were his alibi then. You were also the one who let him out of lockup based on the alibi that girl you've been dating gave. Amy DeLuca, right? The mother of Michael's girlfriend, Maria?"

Valenti shot an angry glance at Bender, who looked slightly sheepish. "What is this sh—"

Hanson interrupted him. "I ain't *done* yet, Jim. Beyond all of this, you were the *only* person who saw Hank Whitmore that night. And *you* were the one who called off the search for him. So it seems to me that—once again— *you're* that kid's alibi."

He paused for a moment, then added, "There's something *weird* been going on between you and that bunch of teenage kids, Guerin included. I'm of the belief that whatever is going on with them is what cost you your job. I don't know what it is, but if you were still sheriff, and all this had happened to one of your deputies, wouldn't *you* be asking some pretty hard questions?"

Valenti started to speak, then snapped his jaw shut. He looked down, then over at Bender, and finally back at Hanson. "It depends on who it was, Randy. There's *some* of you boys I was giving second chances to back when you were having high school keggers and I didn't bust you. All those years I spent in law enforcement, I learned to take the measure of a person, to try to see their worth. Sometimes I was wrong, but I generally knew *who* was worth the extra effort."

He took a step closer to Hanson, and was gratified to see the sheriff flinch almost imperceptibly. "I took that effort with *you*, and look where it's got you now, *Sheriff*. Maybe it's because my son is friends with Michael and the others, or maybe it's because I *still* know who's worth the extra effort. I don't *need* to explain things to you, and the very fact that you're asking shows me that maybe one of those times I judged you, I was *wrong*."

Valenti turned on his heel and stalked toward the stairway up to the ground floor. He had to grit his teeth to resist the urge to punch a hole in the wall on the way out.

Driving home, Valenti rolled Hanson's accusations over and over in his mind. He knew, of course, that Michael Guerin had indeed been responsible for the death of the first man whose charred bones had been found buried in the desert. But that man, FBI Agent Daniel Pierce, had been trying to kill both Valenti and the alien teens; Michael had acted solely in self-defense when he'd killed Pierce, and Valenti had had no alternative but to help Michael and the others cover the incident up.

But the second body was something else entirely. It

crossed Valenti's mind that Michael Guerin certainly had a fine motive for wanting to see Hank Whitmore dead. And that the boy's powers were nearly on a par with Nasedo's, at least in terms of sheer destructiveness.

Still, Valenti didn't want to believe that Michael was capable of murder. *Whoever ends up taking the fall for Whitmore's death,* he thought, *this is all going to end badly.*

8

"Could you have mixed these up any *more*?" Liz looked over at Max, her expression telling him that she was more than slightly frustrated.

"Sorry," he said, shrugging. "I didn't have a lot of time to get the files in the first place. It wasn't like I messed them up on purpose." He lowered his head slightly and smiled gently at her. "What, did you think I did this just so I could spend more time with you?"

Liz put a hand up, palm out. "Just stop with the puppy dog eyes, Mister. I'm not through being mad at you yet."

Boy, is that ever true. The road their relationship had traveled over the past year contained far more potholes and speed bumps than smooth stretches.

"You know, this isn't exactly the type of excitement I was looking for this evening," Liz said.

"It's not evening yet either," Max said, grabbing a handful of the files himself and matching file folder names with the clippings they had contained before he'd dumped them into his Chevy. "We'll have a nice night together after we get done with this. I promise."

"Fine. But this wasn't quite the lunch break I was looking for either," she said, still pouting slightly.

"But these files may contain the key—"

"The key to *everything*," she said, interrupting him. "How many times have I heard *that* one before? Are all aliens such drama queens? Now you're stealing lines from Michael!"

She finished reassembling the contents of one stack of folders and plopped it onto the table. She sat back in the chair, leaning it backward on two legs.

"I'll work on getting some new lines," Max said good-naturedly. He grabbed the diary and notes from Charles Dupree and set them on the corner of the table, out of the declining afternoon sunlight. He pulled one sheet of paper out and pushed it toward Liz. "This is the list of people mentioned by Dupree in his notes. I need your help in checking whether any of them correspond to the names in these files."

Liz leaned back and took the list, scanning it quickly. "How can we be sure that any of these people have anything to do with your genetic codes?"

"We *can't* be," Max said. "But there's a good possibility that some of them might, given that Michael's DNA appears to have come from Dupree. I can't imagine the ship was abducting humans for all that long. There would have been a lot more eyewitnesses."

She shrugged. "The thing I don't understand is why they had to abduct people for *any* extended period of time? Why didn't they just abduct several human beings one day, land the ship, then drop the Pod Squad off in that cave to gestate until it was time to, um, hatch?"

Max put on an exaggerated frown in response to her facetious question. "You're asking me? How would *I* know? Whatever Nasedo and the other aliens were doing, I was still just some little clone zygote of my Antar self when they grabbed Dupree and others. Maybe it took them a while to find the right DNA structure to interact with the alien RNA, or . . . I don't know."

He got up and moved across the rooftop terrace toward the window to Liz's bedroom.

"*Now* where are you going?" Liz's voice went up half an octave. "I'm not going to do all the research work on my own! You always do th—"

"Hey," Max said softly, interrupting her. "I was just going to put some music on while we work." He sat on the windowsill.

"Oh," Liz said simply, then looked down at some of the files on the table as if they were intensely interesting. Max watched a lock of her brown hair escape from the barrettes she used to keep it back while at work. Absentmindedly, she swept it behind her ear. He loved that gesture. It was so Liz.

He opened a black-and-red CD case, slipped the disc into Liz's portable CD player, then punched "play." As he moved back toward the table, the intro began, followed by the entrance of an ethereal female voice that sang a familiar set of lyrics.

"*I didn't hear you leave, I wonder how am I still here? I don't want to move a thing, it might change my memory.*"

Liz looked up at Max, and he grinned sheepishly at her.

"What . . . why did you choose *this* song?" she blustered.

"Because it reminds me of us, of the way things were at the beginning," Max said. "Of the way I wish things could still be."

Liz raised her hands to cover her face, shaking her head. "Aaarrggh! Listen, Max . . ." She looked aside, then shook her head again and looked at him. "I did not bring you up here with me to replay the tortured *Romeo and Juliet* scenes from earlier in our relationship. I brought you up here to help you research this *thing*."

Max smiled at her, nonplussed by her protestations. "So, research it is," he said after a pause. "But can't I enjoy being with you while we do it?"

She stared at him for a moment, and he wasn't sure how she would respond. Her eyes were so round and soulful. Then color crept up into her cheeks as she blushed, and she smiled slyly. "Yeah. I guess there's nothing wrong with that."

"So, can we do some *Romeo and Juliet* tonight?" He grinned.

She pointed a finger at him, squinting with one eye. "Don't push it, E.T. One step at a time."

Both of them smiled as they looked into each other's eyes. Liz finally broke the mutual gaze and resumed looking through the files. Moments later, Max got back to work as well. In the quiet, the music played on.

"I can't breathe, until you're resting here with me . . ."

Half an hour later, Liz put down the set of files she was holding. Her frustration was mounting.

Max stopped shuffling back and forth between folders and looked back at her. Every time he looked at her, Liz felt herself pulled into his eyes. She had shared so much with him, emotionally and mentally. That's why his physical betrayal of her—by sleeping with Tess—had devastated her so.

She knew that she had helped it along a little, by pretending to have slept with Kyle. But that was because the Max from the future had convinced her that a terrible calamity would befall her friends if Max and Liz were to remain together. Still, she had worked the deception out of love, and out of a desire to protect Max.

Liz was reasonably certain he no longer had feelings for Tess, which was the only reason she was allowing him to pull her into his orbit at all. But at times she still wondered if Max's previous bond to Tess had been severed by Tess's recent act of betrayal, when she had taken the Granilith and his unborn son back to Antar to deliver him to Max's enemies. Or maybe her suspicions stemmed from Tess's use of her devious mindwarp ability to cause the death of Alex Whitman and to create problems for the other members of their inner circle. Sometimes Liz wanted to believe that Tess had mindwarped Max into loving her. It made the heartache easier to bear.

"I can't find Dupree's name, or anyone who matches his description in these files," she said, blinking and looking away from Max. "But Dupree's journal mentions some of the names in the files in passing, though none of them seem to match you guys in any physical sense. Of course, half of them don't have pictures, so it's a bit tougher to tell."

"So, we're still at zero then?" Max looked dejected.

"We know that Nasedo and whatever other aliens were aboard the ship were abducting humans," Liz said. "Then they used the Gandarium to cross the DNA of some of those humans with genetic material from the 'Royal Four'—you, Isabel, Michael, and Tess. That combined DNA resulted in two identical sets of four embryos, you guys and the backup set that ended up hatching in New York."

She paused for a second, a new thought slowly simmering in her brain. She tried to bring it quickly to a boil. Then it came to her. "We should be looking for people who *don't* match in these files."

Max looked perplexed. "Huh?"

"Look, you didn't find any files on Charles Dupree at the UFO Center, right?"

Max was still puzzled. "No, but that doesn't mean the files are complete—"

Liz held up a hand to stop him. "Or, it *could* mean that he didn't report his abductions, or that the files got stolen by some of Agent Pierce's people, or any number of things. The point is, his files *aren't* in here."

Max rolled his hand in the air, coaxing Liz to continue. "So, that would mean . . ."

"It means we might be looking in the wrong place. We should look at who *isn't* in the files that *is* mentioned by Dupree in his diary." She looked down the list Max had given her and circled all the names that didn't have notes next to them.

She raised the list in triumph. "Voilà! Three names on here either don't have files, or are definitely eliminated from the list of possible gene donors because of their ethnic backgrounds. That leaves us with three candidates. Darryl Morton. Christine Morton. And Jolene Skarrstin. She was the little girl Dupree mentioned several times in his journal."

"So how do we find them?"

Liz moved over toward the window. "Well, we don't break into the library like you guys are so fond of doing. Not yet, anyhow. First we try the Internet."

As Max left the rooftop to join her inside the house, he moved in close to where she sat at the computer. She could smell him—faint sweat, the peppermint shampoo he used, and a telltale whiff of Tabasco sauce on his breath. *Sweet and sour.* She liked having him this close to her again, wanted to bring him closer, wanted to kiss him . . . but instead, she started typing into the search engines and phone-and-address databases.

Darryl Morton's and Christine Morton's names yielded lots of results separately, but she wasn't able to find any matches that cited both names. She was relatively certain that a name as odd as Jolene Skarrstin's would get some hits, assuming she hadn't married and changed her name. Even then, there might be early records of her.

The screen refreshed, and nineteen citations quickly scrolled onto the screen. "Bingo!"

"You found the farmer's dog?" Max asked with a smile.

She shoved him back, and he fell onto the bed. "Smart aleck. I found Jolene Skarrstin." She clicked on the first listing, which was a notice on one of the University of New Mexico's science bulletin boards. The screen came up, and she saw that it was from the Las Cruces campus. A pang of loss shot through her; that was where Alex had been forced by Tess to decode the alien book. Liz shut her eyes for a moment, swallowed hard, then opened them again to begin reading.

"Anything?" Max asked, peering over her shoulder. She picked up his compelling aroma again, more strongly than usual.

"It appears that Dr. Jolene Skarrstin gave several lectures on genetics recently at the University of New Mexico at Las Cruces. One in January, another last May." She turned to Max, the closeness of their faces making her ache for his kiss. "She works in *genetics*. That's a big clue."

"Let's see what the other Web pages say."

Liz forced herself to stare back at the computer screen and clicked on other citations from the search engine. The second, third, and fourth pages were all variations on the first one. The fifth yielded new information. "She's currently a professor at the University of Santa Fe," she noted.

Liz clicked on the sixth citation. Her computer hung up for a moment, spinning its wheels in cyberspace. She felt Max's breath warm on her ear, and she turned to face him. "Max, we need to—"

"There are pictures," Max blurted out, pointing at the screen. A page about the university faculty party had come up, complete with several pictures of professors and other staff members. Liz read the captions as she scrolled down. As the page moved, a familiar face pixilated into view. Her hair was more gray than blond, and the pearl earrings and dress weren't something Liz could have ever imagined her rival wearing.

The photo caption labeled her as Dr. Jolene Skarrstin.

But the woman in the picture, although clearly in her late fifties or early sixties, was just as clearly Tess Harding.

Liz and Max both gaped at the screen. The room was silent except for the sultry voice of Dido singing in the background and the steady whir of the computer's fan.

The silence was broken moments later as Maria flung the door to Liz's bedroom open, slamming it into the wall.

Liz turned and saw immediately that her friend was frantic. *So what else is new?*

Rising along with Max, she moved toward Maria and looked into her eyes. Liz saw immediately that something was really wrong this time.

"You guys have to come downstairs!" Maria said. "Michael is being arrested! Again!"

9

With her father off to his "appointment"—*definitely* a golf game—and Jesse off on some deposition assignment, Isabel had the entire office to herself. She had already surfed the Internet for a while, but since she wasn't really a Net-head type, the exercise bored her fairly quickly.

Dad's magazines in the waiting area weren't very intriguing either, though she had been interested in an issue of *Entertainment Weekly*. Some starlet whose name she didn't recognize, from some WB show she never watched, still managed to catch her eye, if only for her hair. *I could get mine cut like that. How would I look, though, with longer bangs and everything shorter in the back?*

She'd had long hair all her life. Or at least as far back as she could remember. Even as far back as her emergence from the gestation pod. She had vague recollections of that "birth," of seeing Max for the first time, and later, Michael. Instinctively, she knew that she and Max were alike, and that Michael was different.

Michael is still *different,* she thought. She knew he

hadn't had as good a life as she and Max did growing up. Hank Whitmore was a mean drunk, whereas Phillip and Diane Evans were so wholesome, they almost defined the term *perfect parents*. Isabel knew they weren't perfect; if they were, she and Max would have felt they could tell them the truth about who and what they were. She felt like she knew what gay people must go through, hiding their true selves in the closet for fear others would reject or attack them. Still, Isabel felt that Mom and Dad had been the best parents they could possibly be.

With the few things they had learned about their previous lives on Antar, she knew that Michael was Max's general on that other world. That likely predisposed him toward violence; Isabel wondered how much of his foster father's mean streak might have been integrated into Michael's personality as well.

How much of what we are is predestined? And how much of it do we create ourselves? These questions troubled her of late, especially given the things that Nicholas Crawford—the leader of the alien Skins—had told her about her past life as Vilandra, the supposedly traitorous sister to the king of Antar.

Did I really betray my family and friends? Will I do it again? She felt certain that she could forge her own path—that her destiny was not already written in the stars—though every now and then doubts nagged at her. Especially when she was angry, as she had been toward Max for forbidding her to go to college. Or when she was distraught, as she had been after Alex's death.

Isabel wandered into her father's office and peered out the window, watching the people and cars on the street.

Sometimes she so badly wanted to be just like them.

"You *are* just like them."

The voice startled her, and she turned quickly. There stood Alex, looking just as he had the last time she had seen him alive. Except that he was a ghost. He wasn't real.

"Alex. I didn't hear you come in."

He grinned, then passed his hand through a lamp on her father's desk. "Yeah, well, that's one of the perks of the afterlife. You can kind of appear wherever you want."

"So you *are* a ghost? You're not just some figment of my mind?"

He put a finger up to his lips, as if he was thinking. "Well . . . that's a tough question to answer, isn't it? If I'm a ghost, that means there definitely *is* life after death, which brings up all sorts of issues. But if I'm some expression of your conscience, it means you're actually having a conversation with yourself."

"Oh, how very cryptic, Alex," Isabel said, a pout crossing her face. "Max saw a ghost at Christmas though, so I already *know* there's an afterlife."

"Really? You mean it couldn't have been a manifestation of his guilty conscience, paired with information he gained from some weird alien power still buried in his unconsciousness?" Alex smirked, one eyebrow cocked.

"Ohhhh, you!" Isabel grabbed a pen from the desk and threw it at Alex. It went through him, but hit the pants of Jesse Ramirez, who had just entered the office.

"What did I *do*?" Jesse asked in earnest.

Alex was, of course, gone. Isabel's eyes widened, her hands fluttering in the air. "Oh, I'm so sorry, Jesse. There was a fly in here buzzing around and I was trying to smack it."

He bent over and picked the pen up. "With a pen? Wouldn't a file folder do the job a bit better?"

Isabel was completely embarrassed. "Yeah. Okay, just forget it. I'm sorry I hit you with the pen."

"I'm so wounded," Jesse said, peering around the door-jamb into her father's office, looking for something. She expected he was looking to see if her dad was there. He turned back toward her, grinning. "I know how you can make it up to me."

She sauntered forward until she stood directly in front of him. "And what way would *that* be, Mr. Ramirez?"

He put his arm around her back, pulling her in tighter. "Have dinner with me tonight. Cattleman's Steak House."

"Mmmm, a little too close in," Isabel said. "Somebody might see us." Isabel still wasn't sure how her parents would regard her developing relationship with Jesse; there was no point in advertising it. "How about Hazel's Cajun? It's at least a bit farther away from the office."

"*Oui, mon chère*," Jesse said. "Cajun it is." He bent down and kissed her, wrapping his other arm around her as he did so.

She kissed him back, reveling in the warmth of his lips, allowing her cares and fears to float away. But reality soon intruded on her thoughts, and she wriggled out of his grasp. "Not *here*," she said, admonishing him with a finger. "My dad might walk in at any moment. And besides, your French accent is *horrible*."

Jesse looked up at the ceiling, his arms outstretched. "Twice she wounds me. Why, Lord, why?"

Isabel laughed and returned to the chair behind her desk. She held up the magazine. "So, I'm thinking I should get my hair cut. Do you think I'd look good like this?"

Jesse walked up behind her and swept his hands under her hair, massaging her neck. "Oh no, you won't get me with one of *those* trick questions. That's girl trick number one: Ask what the guy thinks of your hair."

"You are so onto us women," Isabel said. She put her hand up on top of his. "Don't stop. That feels nice."

"Oh, but what if your *dad* walks in?"

"Then I guess we'd have to explain ourselves, wouldn't we?" Isabel responded.

That seemed to cool him off considerably. After a moment or two of silence while he kneaded her shoulders, Jesse said, "You know who *really* needs a haircut is that friend of yours, Michael. He's majorly starting to look like a girl."

Isabel laughed and slapped one of Jesse's hands. "He would *so* hit you if he heard you say that."

"Well, he *does*. What's with the look? Is he purposely trying to get people to think he's a stoner or something?"

"Michael's a good guy," Isabel said. "He's just had a hard life."

Jesse was about to respond when the phone rang. Isabel punched a button and brought the receiver up to her ear. Her voice instantly chirpy, she said, "Good afternoon, Evans Law Office. How may I help you?" The expression on her face changed quickly. "Slow down, Max. They're doing what? *Again*? What are the charges? He's not here right now. Hold—okay, *hold on* a minute."

She swiveled her chair and looked up at Jesse. "Speak of the devil. Two deputies just came to arrest Michael at the Crashdown."

"Good guy, huh?" Jesse said with a questioning look.

"Jesse—just *trust* me on this. Dad isn't here, but he's worked as Michael's lawyer before, *pro bono*. I'd call him, but I don't think his cell phone is on. Will you help?"

He hesitated for just a bit before nodding. "If you want me to, I will."

"Thanks," she said, then turned back to the phone. "Jesse and I will get down to the station right away. *Jesse Ramirez*. The new lawyer. I'm *sure* I told you about him. Look, just tell Michael not to say—oh, he's already gone? Well, he's got a lot of experience with being arrested. He probably knows not to say or do anything stupid. Okay, Max, let me go."

She hung up the phone, hastily scribbled a few words of explanation onto a sticky note, then slapped the message onto the door of her father's office, partially closing it.

Grabbing her cell phone, she dialed her father's wireless number. After four rings, his voice-mail picked up. "Dad, it's Isabel. Michael Guerin's been arrested again. Jesse—*Mr. Ramirez*—and I are going down to the sheriff's station now. Bye."

After scooping up a pen and a yellow legal pad from her desk, she turned back toward Jesse, who was waiting expectantly by the door. "Thank you for doing this. It means a lot to me." She kissed him quickly on the lips, then turned toward the door. "Come on. You're driving."

Jesse stooped to pick up his briefcase. "What did they arrest him for?"

Her hand on the doorknob, Isabel turned. "They think he murdered his foster father."

10

Sunset was still a couple of hours away. The evening shift was just settling in when Valenti strode into the reception area. He asked Deputy Blackwood if Sheriff Hanson was in, and wasn't at all surprised to find that his young go-getter replacement was busying himself with the endless minutiae of the job, carrying a thick stack of hard-copy files from the records room toward his office. *Too bad I never taught that boy to delegate,* Valenti thought. *Maybe he needs a hobby.*

Valenti also wasn't surprised at Hanson's scowl when he announced that he wanted to speak with Michael Guerin. Immediately.

"I'm not sure that's such a good idea, Jim."

"Come on, Randy," Valenti said, following Hanson into his office. "What possible reason do you have to shut me out? Unless *you're* the one who has something to hide."

Plopping the files down on a corner of the desk, Hanson sat behind it and removed his sheriff's hat. Valenti noticed that the younger man was unconsciously squeezing the cowboy-style hat into a pretzel shape before he realized what he was doing and set it aside.

"All right, Jim. Have it your way," Hanson said before leaning forward and pressing the intercom button. "Deputy Blackwood, would you escort the Guerin boy to my office?"

"Sure thing, Randy," said the voice on the other end of the line.

Perhaps a minute later, Blackwood appeared at the door, a sullen Michael standing at his side. Michael's hands were cuffed before him, and rings of worry darkened his eyes. But his expression remained defiant.

Hang in there, Valenti thought as Blackwood returned to the reception area, leaving Michael alone with the two men. Valenti considered how much simpler it would be to exonerate Michael if he could simply come clean about the lad's alien nature. Unfortunately, that simply wasn't an option. *This is all going to work out, kid. Just as long as you don't let them bait you into saying anything stupid before I can get you a lawyer.*

"You wanted to talk to him?" Hanson said, folding his arms and glowering at the boy. "Here he is."

"Thanks, Randy. Now if we could have a bit of privacy. . . ."

Shaking his head, Hanson turned toward Valenti. "No can do, Jim. Not unless you can show me papers saying you're either his priest, his lawyer, or his legal guardian. Otherwise, whatever you two have to say to each other you can say in front of me." He paused for a moment, then added, "You're not the sheriff anymore, Jim."

A snarl on his lips, Michael started to open his mouth,

no doubt readying a withering rejoinder for the sheriff. But he stopped when he locked eyes with Valenti.

Standing beside the desk where Hanson sat, the ex-sheriff mouthed a silent *DON'T TELL HIM ANYTHING* to Michael. Hanson, who had been watching Michael, must have seen a flicker of reaction on the boy's face.

"All right," Hanson said, jerking his head back toward Valenti. He rose, moved to the door, and half opened it. "I can't have you two trying to slip each other messages behind my back. Go home, Jim."

So Hanson's going to push me, Valenti thought, a tide of anger raising within him. He decided he had little to lose by pushing back.

"Dammit, Randy, I taught you everything you know about wearing that badge. Don't get all high-hat with me now. Makes you look like Barney Fife."

Hanson hooked his thumbs into his leather belt, obviously making a show of placing a hand near his revolver. "I asked you nicely, Jim. Don't force me to make it an order."

"Don't act like this is the gunfight at the O.K. Corral. I came here to talk to Michael, not to get into pissing contests over who's in charge around here."

"I'm the one in charge around here," Hanson growled. "Don't forget that. Good night, Jim."

Michael was beginning to look uncharacteristically apprehensive. "Maybe we ought to try this again tomorrow," he said to Valenti.

"Shut up, Mr. Guerin," Valenti said, never moving his eyes from Hanson. "The grown-ups are talking now, son."

Hanson sighed in frustration, throwing up his hands. He had evidently realized that Valenti wasn't going anywhere, unless physically coerced. However confident Hanson seemed, Valenti sensed that the young sheriff wasn't willing to go quite that far in butting heads with his old boss.

"I don't get it, Jim. Why do you keep walking through fire for these damned kids? You've already lost your career over them. How much further are you gonna go with this?"

Valenti smiled grimly, but said nothing. *As far as I have to, I suppose,* he thought.

The office door, which had stood ajar, suddenly opened completely. Blackwood stood in the hallway, flanked by Isabel Evans and a dark-complected, well-dressed, briefcase-toting young man. Valenti thought he'd seen him around town, but couldn't quite place him. But the young man's attire and manner said lawyer quite clearly.

So somebody's already found Michael an attorney. Good. That's one more thing I can scratch off today's 'to do' list.

"What the hell is it now, Owen?" Hanson snapped, plainly annoyed by the intrusion. Valenti smiled wryly as he watched his successor's fit of temper. *Keeping one's cool, he knew, was an integral part of a sheriff's job. The kid'll get the hang of it eventually. Look how far he's already come.*

"More visitors for the prisoner," Blackwood said, scowling. Valenti assumed that the big deputy would call his boss on the carpet later on for barking at him, when no one was around to listen in. Blackwood had always been a gentle soul, but he'd never suffered either fools or unfairness gladly, and it wasn't a good idea to get on his bad side—even if you were the boss. Valenti knew that Randy would apologize for his gaffe, sooner or later.

The well-dressed young man stepped forward into the office and shook Hanson's hand. "Good evening, Sheriff. I'm Jesse Ramirez, from the Evans Law Office. I'll be advocating on behalf of Mr. Guerin."

"Does this mean I finally get to talk now?" Michael said, scratching his face. The handcuffs made the maneuver awkward.

Valenti glared at him. "No," he said, in unison with both Ramirez and Isabel.

"Do you have a room where I can speak with my client?" Ramirez asked, hefting his small briefcase.

Hanson nodded, quickly recovering his composure. "Deputy Blackwood will show you to one of the conference rooms."

Ramirez and Isabel started to follow Blackwood back into the hallway when Hanson stopped them. "Wait a minute, miss. You're Isabel Evans, aren't you? One of Michael's school friends."

"Yes, that's right," she said, clutching her legal pad before her.

"I have no problem letting Mr. Ramirez have a private interview with the prisoner," Hanson said. "But I'm gonna have to ask you to wait outside, miss."

Isabel frowned, holding up the pad. "My father won't

be very happy if you inconvenience Mr. Ramirez. He's not here to take down all his own notes."

"Time is money," Ramirez said, flashing a disarming smile. "That's why Phillip Evans loaned me one of his best paralegals to take Mr. Guerin's deposition."

Valenti couldn't quite stifle a smile as he watched a Curses! Foiled again! expression crumple across Hanson's brow. Michael exchanged a quick grin with Isabel.

Hanson evidently caught some of the nonverbal byplay out of the corner of his eye. He was unamused. "All right. Go swear out your deposition."

"Thank you, Sheriff," Ramirez said. Blackwood escorted him, Isabel, and Michael out into the hall.

Hanson closed the door, then walked over to Valenti. The young sheriff's brow remained furrowed. "I know you're convinced that the Guerin boy is innocent, Jim. In spite of the fact that this is his third arrest, I might add."

"He's a misunderstood kid, Randy. He's had a harder life than most. Every one of his previous arrests has been tossed out. And he's certainly no killer."

Hanson folded his arms and leaned against his desk. "So you've been saying all along. But for an innocent man, don't you think he 'lawyered up' kind of fast?"

His jaw muscles working involuntarily, Valenti left Hanson's office without responding.

"How the hell can they keep me here?" Michael said, rage seething in his guts. He leaned backward in his chair, rubbing at his wrists, which chafed slightly where the handcuffs had been before Blackwood had removed them. "All

I know about my useless late foster dad is that he ran away from home. Good riddance."

"Apparently he vanished at about the same time you moved out of his trailer and became a legally emancipated minor," Ramirez said. He sat on the other side of a long wooden table whose top was scarred by years of use. Seated beside him, Isabel scribbled notes on her pad while Ramirez's small tape machine quietly recorded the proceedings.

This guy doesn't like me, Michael thought, looking Ramirez up and down. The young lawyer's fine wool suit immediately put him on edge, a reminder of all of the privileges he'd had to do without throughout his young life. *He might have taken me on as a charity case to make Isabel happy, but he still thinks I'm some sort of guilty-until-proven-innocent lowlife.*

"What are you saying?" Michael said. "That they're right? That I killed Hank Whitmore?"

Ramirez stroked his smooth chin thoughtfully. His tone was infuriatingly calm. "Did you?"

"Jesse!" said Isabel. Her pen clattered to the tabletop.

"I'm only asking the kind of questions he's gonna hear in front of the grand jury, Isabel. He'd better get used to it right now."

Michael stood up, fighting down an urge to kick Ramirez's too-perfect teeth down his throat. "That's it. You're fired. Thank you for coming. I'll take my chances with the public defender's office."

"Sit down," Ramirez said, his easy manner giving way to a hard tone of authority. "I'm not the one accusing you here. The state of New Mexico is, and based on the circumstantial evidence—and your past record—you may have more than a little explaining to do."

Michael remained standing, eyeing the tony lawyer suspiciously. "What's in it for you?"

Ramirez smiled, displaying his too-even, too-white teeth. Michael wondered how much he'd paid to get them to look that way. "Besides fortune and glory? Listen, kid. I don't know much more about you than what I read in your previous arrest reports—and what Isabel told me about you during the drive over. She says that Whitmore used to beat you up."

Michael scowled at Isabel. "Thanks for the character testimony, Iz. Now they'll throw away the key."

She stuck out her tongue at him and resumed jotting down notes.

"I want to help you, Michael," Ramirez continued. "I used to work as an intern in the public defender's office. I've seen what a crapshoot indigent clients get—"

Michael interrupted him. "Who're you calling *indigent*?" His hands clenched into fists unconsciously. "I have a job and an apartment."

Ramirez didn't miss a beat. "Face reality, Michael. You're not exactly society page material, even by trailer park standards. But Isabel is a pretty good judge of character. And if she says you're not guilty, then that's good enough for me. For her sake, I'm not going to leave your fate in the hands of some underpaid, overworked, and possibly alcoholic P.D. who just might end up sleeping through your trial."

My God! He thinks this is going to go to trial! Michael

could feel alien energies beginning to build up deep within his chest, unbidden. With a supreme effort of will, he forced them down. But his anger and frustration continued to smolder just below the surface. He desperately wanted to blast something apart.

Isabel must have sensed his interior struggle. "Please, Michael," she said, looking up from her pad with pleading eyes. "Take a deep breath and sit down, before you keel over from testosterone poisoning. We're both trying to help you."

Michael began to realize that Ramirez was right. He couldn't afford to hire a decent lawyer on his own. He could barely afford to pay his rent on what he made flipping burgers at the Crashdown; he had even been considering taking a second job. He decided to accept that his best hope of getting out of this was to trust this smarmy young lawyer.

He sat, though he remained unable to force the sullen expression from his face. "All right. What do you need me to do?"

"All right," Ramirez said. "We need to account for your whereabouts right before, during, and after the time Sheriff Valenti said he'd seen Whitmore for the last time."

"I spent a lot of time working at the Crashdown. And hanging around with Maria, Max, Isabel, Liz, Kyle, and Alex."

"Hmmm," Ramirez said. "The usual suspects, and always thick as thieves. I can see I've got my work cut out for me."

Isabel shot a sour look in Ramirez's direction, then

looked Michael squarely in the eye. "What *can* you tell us about Hank Whitmore's disappearance, Michael?"

"Pretty much nothing," Michael said, shaking his head. "I spent part of those last few days with your dad, doing the paperwork to get myself legally emancipated. And I had to get busy searching for an apartment."

"So you had to move your things from Whitmore's trailer to your new place," Ramirez said. "Did you see your foster father at all during that time?"

"No. After I was emancipated, I never saw Hammerin' Hank again. When I dropped by the trailer to pick up my stuff, I figured he'd just gone off on another bender. But I guess he was already gone by then. Or maybe he was even dead already."

Ramirez rose to his feet, then shut off the recorder. "All right, Michael. I'm beginning to think that we've got a good chance of getting these charges summarily dismissed at your hearing tomorrow. *Unless* somebody's found the proverbial smoking gun lying right next to Whitmore's body. But I think I'd already know about that if anybody had."

Michael and Isabel also rose. "So what am I supposed to do between now and the hearing?"

"Do?" Ramirez said as he packed his recorder back into the briefcase. "Nothing. And be quiet."

"In other words," Isabel said, "don't say anything stupid. And for Pete's sake, don't *do* anything stupid."

Michael smiled wryly. *Right. If I used my powers to blow a hole in my cell and escape, I guess I'd look pretty guilty.*

Aloud, he said, "It's hard to just sit here while the real killer could still be running around out there somewhere."

Ramirez looked imploringly heavenward, shaking his head. "You've watched too many reruns of *The Fugitive.*" Looking Michael straight in the eye, he said, "You need to worry about not doing anything to make your situation any worse that it already is, Mr. Guerin. Let somebody else worry about catching the one-armed man, okay?"

Isabel nodded in agreement. "Besides, I'm not sure we're completely positive that Whitmore was murdered. Couldn't he have died in an accident of some kind?"

Michael scowled. "Sure. First, his Coleman stove accidentally burns him to Crispy Critters while he's camping. Then he accidentally buries himself. Sheriff Hanson told me the body turned up in a shallow grave out in the desert someplace, burned up like it had been in a fire. Guess he was trying to Dennis Franz a confession out of me."

Ramirez blanched, evidently unaware of the grisly details of Whitmore's death. *Wuss,* Michael thought.

"So somebody really *did* kill him," Isabel said, evidently thinking aloud. "It's just a matter of finding out who."

And I've got a pretty good idea who it is, Michael thought. *Or who it was.*

But there was no way to give voice to his growing suspicion. Not with Ramirez in the room.

Then an inspiration seized him. Drawing a single quick breath, Michael covered his nose and mouth, went into a theatrical-looking windup, and issued a loud, fake sneeze: *Na-SE-do!*

Locking eyes with Isabel, Michael saw that she understood his meaning—Nasedo, the late shape-shifter, could have used his powers to fry Whitmore, no doubt to protect him from the drunken fool's recurrent fits of rage.

"Bless you," Isabel said just before they exited the room.

Blackwood immediately returned, cuffed him, then escorted him back to the dingy little jail cell. There, he removed the cuffs and left Michael alone with his thoughts. *Try to keep them pleasant,* Michael told himself, sitting on one of the cell's two lumpy cots. Watching the shadows of the bars gradually lengthen across the floor as the afternoon wore on toward evening, he felt grateful that he didn't yet have to share the place with a roommate.

Yeah. Think pleasant thoughts. He looked down at his hands. *And try not to blow any holes in the walls.*

As Isabel headed across the station's parking lot with Jesse toward his car, a familiar vehicle pulled into a parking space beside them.

"Dad!" said Isabel, overjoyed to see Phillip Evans stepping out of the car, still wearing his golf pants and polo shirt. She could see the bag of golf clubs lying askew across the backseat, obviously placed there in haste.

"I came as soon as I got your message about Michael," Mr. Evans said to Isabel.

At that moment, Max's Chevy roared into the lot, coming to a crooked stop two spaces away from Evans's car. Max and Maria jumped out and ran to join the group.

"Easy there, Racer X," Isabel said.

"Sorry it took us so long," Max said. "Maria needed to spend some time shouting at the skies and breaking things before I'd risk getting into a car with her."

Maria glowered. "Watch it, buster. I might not be through breaking things yet."

"Where's Liz?" Isabel wondered aloud.

"Somebody had to hold down the fort back at the Crashdown," Maria said. Isabel noticed only then that Maria hadn't taken the time to change out of her garish, lime green waitress outfit. The spring-mounted "alien antennae" dingleballs that completed her costume bobbled back and forth over her head whenever she spoke or moved.

Taking Isabel aside for a moment, Max whispered, "Jim Valenti left me a message a few hours ago about a body Hanson dug up out in the desert. And Maria said that Hanson's deputies picked up Michael and accused him of murdering Hank Whitmore. That *can't* be a coincidence."

"It's not," Isabel said. "Now we just need to figure out what to do about it."

"Valenti thinks Nasedo might have been involved in the murder," Max said, his voice still pitched only for Isabel's ears.

Isabel nodded. "That's what Michael thinks, too. It's the only explanation that makes any sense."

Max leaned in closer, obviously not wanting to be over-heard. "Something else important has come up too. Liz and I have just come across a lead on finding Tess's genetic template."

Isabel's mind whirled. "The human abductee who supplied Tess's DNA?"

"That's what we think. We're leaving tonight to track her down. She might be able to lead us to *our* genetic templates. I've called Kyle already, and he's coming with me. We'll need your help too, to see whether or not this woman is the real deal."

She started to protest. "Max—"

"We *have* to talk to her," he interrupted. "We have to learn whatever she might remember about her abduction. We have to find out what she knows. She's a genetics researcher."

"Max, Michael is in *real* trouble. You can't just bail on him to chase *Tess*."

Max made a sour face. "I'm not 'bailing,' Isabel. And I'm not chasing *Tess*. Maria and I rushed right over here just as soon as we could. But once we're done rescuing Michael— *again*—we need to head for Santa Fe to find this woman."

"Max, you're not being fair to Michael. This arrest was no more his fault than having that creep Hank Whitmore for a foster father was."

Max looked exasperated. "Fine! Isabel, this woman in Santa Fe could provide the key to finding out literally *everything* we don't know yet about our past. . . ." He trailed off, his eyes unfocused as he stared off into the cloudless sky. Isabel saw the look of longing in her brother's dark eyes. He obviously felt a desperate need to unravel the mystery of their origins. And she couldn't deny that she often felt the same need as well.

"All right, Max," she said. "I'm in. I have some dinner plans, though, so I'd like to leave a little later on this evening, if that's okay with you. But let's take first things first, okay?"

Placing her hand on Max's arm, Isabel propelled him back toward their father. Moving close to Jesse, Isabel saw that her father was speaking to him. She also noticed that Jesse appeared to be taking great care not to touch her, even by accident. Maria appeared to be listening closely to the conversation between the lawyers, while impatiently shifting her weight from foot to foot.

"How bad does Michael's situation really look, Jesse?" Mr. Evans asked.

Jesse absently drummed on his briefcase as he answered. "There are pluses and minuses here. In the plus column, Hanson doesn't seem to have a shred of hard evidence placing Michael near the scene of the crime. On the minus side, Whitmore used to use the kid for a punching bag. And his only alibi comes from a handful of teenagers, who a judge might think are lying to protect him." He looked around at everyone assembled before adding, "No offense."

Mr. Evans nodded, weighing the younger lawyer's words. "So Michael appears to have an excellent motive for killing Whitmore, at least on paper."

Isabel couldn't believe what she was hearing. "Daddy! What are you saying? You can't honestly believe that Michael would—"

Her father interrupted her, placing a calming arm around her shoulder. "Honey, I never would have helped Michael get emancipated if I'd judged him capable of committing murder."

"I know he didn't do it," she said. Tears pooled in her eyes.

"I'll vouch for him, too," Maria said. She still seemed oblivious to the antennae projecting from her forehead, which described incredibly complex patterns in the air as she spoke and gesticulated. "Michael might be hotheaded, impulsive, insensitive, emotionally tone-deaf, and possibly the worst boyfriend ever to drag his knuckles through the hallowed halls of West Roswell High, but he's no *murderer*."

"What Maria said," Max said.

"All right," Mr. Evans said, smiling wryly. "But that boy could run up some pretty princely legal bills before this business is finished."

"I've already offered to handle the case on a pro bono basis, sir," said Jesse, exchanging a quick smile with Isabel. "Entirely on my own time, if necessary."

"No," Mr. Evans said.

"No?" Isabel said. Her heart sank. Maria looked like she was about to detonate. Max watched quietly.

"I said 'no' and I meant 'no.' The *Evans Law Office* is taking the case pro bono." Mr. Evans shook Jesse's hand. "Every resource you might need for this case will be at your disposal, Counselor. I'll stand behind you completely. Full faith and credit, and all that,"

"Thank you, Daddy," Isabel said, hugging her father tightly.

"Yes," Maria said, piling onto the hug. "Thankyouthankyouthankyouthankyou."

"Kids? Need . . . air," Phillip Evans gasped. Isabel released her grip and took a step back, smiling at her father, who was feigning strangulation in Maria's grateful, octopus-like embrace.

Suddenly self-conscious, Maria backed away as well. Then she grabbed the senior lawyer's hand, pumping it up and down like a farmer trying to get water out of a cistern. The antenna-dingleballs atop her head continued to dance crazily to and fro. Jesse watched, his eyes spinning like tiny pinwheels.

I've really got to talk that girl into switching to decaf, Isabel thought.

"How can they hold him without any real evidence?" Max asked, pulling the antennae from Maria's head and then handing them back to her without so much as glancing in her direction.

Mr. Evans sighed wearily. "I called Sheriff Hanson on the way over. I admit he's a little overeager. But he really believes he has probable cause to hold Michael."

"But Michael's completely *innocent!*" Isabel said.

Twisting her amputated antennae nervously in her hands, Maria jumped in. "And contrary to all his press, he is very fragile emotionally. A night in jail is a trauma he shouldn't have to endure right now." She paused, looking sheepish. "Um, *another* night in jail, I mean."

Looking glum, Mr. Evans turned toward Isabel. "Hanson says he thinks Michael will skip town if he sets the boy free. He's determined to hang on to him until tomorrow's hearing in Judge Lewis's courtroom. And I don't think anything short of an order from Lewis himself will change the sheriff's mind."

"Lewis. Great. The Hanging Judge," complained Maria. "He's the guy who chopped Sheriff Valenti's head off last year. The soul of compassion. He's got a sign on his bench that says 'cruel, but fair.'"

"I've known Judge Lewis for twenty years," Mr. Evans said, chuckling. "He's a good man, and an even-tempered jurist."

"Michael won't run," Max said. "I can guarantee it."

Jesse shook his head. "He's left town suddenly before.

Why are you so sure he'll stay put this time?"

Because if he was going to run away he'd already have blasted his way out of his cell by now, Isabel thought.

She observed that Max appeared to be thinking the same thing. "I just am," he said.

"Me too," Maria said. "I'll quote you chapter and verse on why I think so, if you'd like. In fact—"

"That's okay," Mr. Evans said, splaying his hands out before him as though warding off an attack. "Really."

Isabel looked imploringly in her father's direction. "You *believe* Michael is innocent, don't you?"

Mr. Evans didn't hesitate. "Of course I do, honey. But that might not be enough."

Isabel wasn't about to give up so easily. "There has to be something you can do to get Michael out of jail today."

Mr. Evans paused, evidently considering his options. Then he kissed his adopted daughter on the forehead and pulled his cell phone from his belt. "I hope you haven't made any plans for this evening, Jesse," he said as he began keying in a number.

Jesse looked at Isabel helplessly. "Um, no. Why?"

Crap, Isabel thought. *So much for an intimate dinner together at Hazel's Cajun.*

"Because," Evans said, "we're both going to pay Sheriff Hanson a visit. And I think we're going to have to do a bit of paperwork while we're there."

"Why?" Jesse asked, nonplussed.

"Because Hanson's about to receive an urgent request from a certain highly influential 'cruel-but-fair' jurist." Mr. Evans held the phone up to his ear. "Judge Lewis? Phillip Evans here. I have a personal favor to ask of you. . . ."

11

About ninety minutes after Phillip Evans had placed his phone call to Judge Lewis, Maria was running, holding Michael's hand, pulling him along behind her. She enjoyed a heady thrill of triumph as she bounded across her driveway, past the spot where Liz had left Maria's Jetta parked. The car made slight pinging sounds as its engine slowly cooled to match the temperature of the warm, early evening air. Dusk was gathering quickly.

Maria sailed through the front door, a sulky Michael still in tow. "Lucy, I'm home!"

As she'd expected, Liz Parker was already inside waiting for her, sitting on the sofa and leafing through a magazine. Unlike Maria, Liz had already doffed her lime green Crashdown uniform in favor of jeans and a loose, white cotton blouse, no doubt having run up to her little flat above the restaurant before driving Maria's car over to the house.

"So was this a jailbreak?" Liz said, her facing brimming with happiness. "Or did you just sweet-talk Sheriff Hanson into letting Michael out? You didn't give me a lot of the details when you called."

"It was Max's dad," Michael said, sounding considerably less happy than Liz. "He was the one who rescued me." Maria thought the phrase "this time" was hanging unuttered in the air, completing Michael's sentence as he lapsed into a sullen silence.

Seeing that her half-alien boyfriend's monosyllabic storytelling technique wasn't satisfying Liz, Maria jumped in. "Mr. Evans called in some favors to spring Michael. It turns out that he and Judge Lewis are old friends. So Michael is free until his hearing tomorrow." Maria looked expectantly toward Michael. "As long as you don't get picked up for anything else in the meantime."

"I promised Deputy Dawg I'd stay out of trouble," Michael said, sounding miffed. "And I will."

"Care to discuss the trouble you're *already* in, Spaceboy?" said Maria. It occurred to her that she'd been made aware of very little about the case, other than Hanson's suspicions that Michael might have caused the death of Hank Whitmore.

"There's nothing to discuss," he said, folding his arms, his bangs half covering his eyes. "Hanson's just assumed the worst about me, the way people around here generally do. The fact that none of it's true doesn't seem to matter much. Again, par for the course."

She took his hand, partly to provide comfort and partly to forestall yet another "woe is me" Michael pity party. "We'll straighten it all out tomorrow. At the hearing."

Michael looked like he wanted to smash something, but appeared to be restraining himself—just barely—to avoid enraging Maria's mom, Amy. Maria knew that there were some perils that not even the commanding general of the armed forces of the planet Antar would willingly risk facing.

"Judge Lewis," Michael said with a defeated sigh. "Great. I should save everybody some time and go get measured for my orange jumpsuit right now."

Maria made a show of looking at her watch, then shook her head theatrically at Michael. "Sorry, Michael. All the haberdasheries are closed at this hour."

"Lewis evidently believed in you enough to go to bat for you with Hanson," Liz said. "Mr. Evans couldn't have forced that on him, even if they *are* old friends. So maybe the hearing won't go as badly as you think."

Michael didn't appear convinced. "Maybe. But I find that when I count on not getting cut any slack, I'm usually not disappointed."

"Michael, I would bet *real* money that Eeyore was your favorite Winnie the Pooh character," Maria said.

He snorted. "Eeyore was the only pragmatic realist in the entire Hundred Acre Wood."

Let's hear it for the power of positive thinking, Maria thought with a mental shrug. *Oh, well. Michael will be Michael.*

"If you're really that worried about Judge Lewis not treating you fairly," Liz said, "then why don't you try to even the odds a little?"

Michael frowned. "What do you mean?"

Liz went to the couch and took her cell phone from her purse. "Let's talk to somebody who has some firsthand experience with the judge," Liz said.

"Jim Valenti," Maria said, instantly understanding Liz's plan.

Michael shook his head. "Lewis is the one who suspended Valenti as sheriff. If not for him, the city council might never have voted to give him the boot."

"Exactly," Maria said. "And that experience probably gave Valenti all sorts of insights into Lewis's legal mind. A real peek beneath the robes, so to speak."

"Great," Michael said. "There's an image that'll haunt me in the middle of the night."

"It might keep your mind off jail," Liz said, studying Michael's pouting profile. She walked away and had a brief conversation with Valenti.

Speaking to Maria, Liz said, "I just told Valenti that Michael's over here, and that he could use a strategy session for tomorrow's hearing—"

"You mean inquisition," Michael interrupted.

"Whatever," said Liz, casting an exasperated look at Michael. "Anyway, he's on his way over now to help us make our game plan for tomorrow."

"Good," Maria said to Liz. "I've just gotta believe that Michael's release is a good omen. I admit, I wasn't sure it was actually going to work—asking Judge Lewis to lean on Hanson to free Michael. I don't think I really believed Mr. Evans had pulled it off until we were all piling into Max's car out in the parking lot."

Liz brightened. "Max brought you home?"

"Yeah," Maria said. *Uh-oh.* Because of Michael's dismal record of pulling unexpected disappearing acts, Maria understood exactly how Liz felt.

"If Max drove you home, then why didn't he stop in? He must have heard you talking to me on your cell phone. So he *knew* I was here."

"You know Max," Maria said, shrugging. "Sometimes he can be very . . . focused. The only thing I can't quite figure out is exactly *what* he's focused on this time." She looked to Michael, her eyebrows rising.

Michael looked uncomfortable, and appeared to be considering what he was going to say very carefully. At length, he said, "Max and Isabel had some, um, urgent business to take care of."

Maria nodded knowingly. "Urgent *Czechoslovakian* business?"

"No comment," Michael said, then turned to stone.

Liz turned on Michael. "Where did they go?" she said, a small burr of anger texturing her usually smooth voice.

"They went north," Michael said after a pause, his expression still guarded.

"*Where* north?"

"Santa Fe."

Watching the stubborn set of Michael's jaw, Maria sighed and shook her head. "Better get out the rubber hose and the thumbscrews, Liz. Otherwise you're only gonna get his name, rank, and serial number."

Liz's brow furrowed. "Santa Fe? But Max and I were going to go to the movies tonight."

"Not anymore," Michael said. Maria thought he looked nearly as unhappy as Liz did.

Maria offered Liz a sympathetic look. "I'm sorry, sweetie," she said before turning toward Michael and throwing her arms around him. "And I hereby take back everything I ever said about you being the world's worst Significant Other, Spaceboy."

"Thanks. I think." Michael gave her a perfunctory squeeze, then disengaged himself from the embrace. He seemed to be withdrawing into one of his sullen *I-really-don't-want-to-be-touched-right-now* moods. Without bothering to ask Maria's permission, he flopped onto the couch, picked up the TV remote, and started surfing the channels. His finger came to rest just as a blue-faced Mel Gibson led a ragtag Scots army into a bloody battle against the English.

Maria took a step back and studied Michael's tormented expression. A realization suddenly came to her. "I think I get it now, Michael. You're disappointed because you have to stay here with me. What you *really* wanted to do was go with Max and Isabel to Santa Fe."

Before Michael could respond, Liz smacked herself on the forehead. "Skarrstin!"

"Gesundheit," Maria said.

"No, *Jolene* Skarrstin."

"And who, pray tell, is Jolene Skarrstin?" Maria asked.

"Someone Max and I were researching on the Internet earlier today. She's a genetics professor at the University of Santa Fe."

"Okay," Maria said, still clueless as to where this all was headed. "So you were cyber-stalking some college professor because . . . ?"

Liz's frown deepened. "Because Max thinks she may be the person whose DNA was used to create Tess."

Maria watched Liz cross to the speaker phone on the coffee table in front of the sofa. Michael looked irritated when Liz got in the way of the screen as she began placing a call on speaker.

"Max!" Liz said moments later, nearly shouting into the speaker. "I know you and Isabel are on your way to find this Dr. Skarrstin person in Santa Fe."

"I'm here too," said a second, fainter male voice on the other end of the line. Maria recognized Kyle Valenti's voice, despite the drone of road noise that competed with it.

Upset, Liz didn't bother to acknowledge Kyle. "Max, I thought we were going to the movies tonight."

Max sounded sheepish. "Sorry, Liz. I guess I forgot. Tonight seemed like the best opportunity to head out for Santa Fe, now that everyone's attention is focused on Michael instead of on Isabel and me."

"Happy to be of help, Maxwell," Michael said wryly, not taking his eyes off the screen.

Max continued. "We told our parents we were going to a concert and staying in Santa Fe overnight."

"I guess it's always best to stay as close to the truth as possible when lying to parents," Maria said.

"And I told my dad," Kyle said, evidently having just borrowed the phone from Max, "that we were tracking down Tess Harding's human gene donor so we could ask her some questions and maybe settle the basic existential questions of existence for you Pod Squad people."

Maria's eyebrows shot up, along with the pitch of her voice. "You just told him the *truth*? And he was *okay* with that?"

"Given how many concerts he's seen get out of hand during his years as sheriff, he would have been a lot more worried about me if I'd used Max's cover story."

"Fair enough," Maria said, remembering a few of her own harrowing mosh-pit experiences.

"I could have helped," Liz said softly, sounding hurt.

It must have taken a moment for Kyle to pass the phone back to Max. "I didn't want Maria to have to baby-sit Michael all by herself," Max said after a brief beat.

Michael answered that with a loud, long Bronx cheer.

Isabel's voice came on the line next. "What was that? I couldn't quite make that out."

"That was Michael," Maria said. "He just said he wishes you all luck in getting hold of this Dr. Starsky person."

"Skarrstin," Liz corrected.

"Whatever."

"Fine, Max. Good luck. Try to stay out of trouble. That goes for all of you," Liz said.

Kyle was back on the line a moment later. "We're going to interview a little old lady from Santa Fe, Liz. It's not like we're hot on the corpse-strewn trail of Nasedo."

Maria had to admit that Kyle had a point. The world wasn't entirely populated by Men in Black or shape-changing alien serial killers. Indiana Jones aside, most university professors weren't the reckless, dangerous types.

Liz hung up without bothering to say good-bye. The room was silent, except for the television.

Liz looked as though she couldn't decide whether she wanted to break something or burst into tears.

"You okay?" Maria asked.

"I'm fine."

"No. You're not."

"Okay, I'm not. But I will be. Once I sort out what's

going on between me and Max. Or whether anything *is* going on between us. And how mad I'm allowed to get at him until I figure the rest of it out."

Max stood her up again, Maria thought. *And for Tess, of all the other people in the universe he could possibly have thrown Liz over for. That has got to hurt.*

Knowing there was nothing she could say to comfort her friend, Maria drew Liz into a gentle, sympathetic hug.

At that moment, a loud knock sounded on the front door, startling all three of them. Maria opened the door and saw Jim Valenti standing on the porch, his expression serious. She quickly invited him in.

Entering, Valenti quickly scanned the living room and said quick "hellos" to the three teens. Michael offered him a perfunctory wave, though his eyeballs remained enslaved by the tube

"Is Amy around?" Valenti asked, walking back toward the still-open door. He glanced out at the street, looking like a man who thought he was being followed.

"Not yet," Maria said. "She's still at the store."

Valenti nodded, looking relieved. He closed the door and walked back to the center of the living room. "Well, as long as your mom is elsewhere, that ought to make it easier for us to discuss what we have to discuss." Everyone present knew that Amy DeLuca, Maria's mother and the owner of Roswell's most famous alien-themed gift shop, was no more aware of the Pod Squad's alien origins than Phillip and Diane Evans were.

"Are you ready to start planning for tomorrow's hearing, Michael?" Valenti said. "Or should I just go into the kitchen and make you some popcorn?"

Michael pushed himself into an upright position on the couch, pointed the remote, and killed the TV. "I guess I should thank you for trying to help me," he said.

Valenti said, "Probably. But let's take things one step at a time. First, I want to clear the air of one very important thing."

"All right," Michael said, looking as stoic as ever.

"I've looked at Whitmore's body at the morgue, and from what I saw I can safely conclude that alien powers killed him. It couldn't have been anything else. I didn't know you were an alien when your stepdad disappeared. Nor did I know anything about Nasedo back then. So I have to start by asking you one question, Michael. And I want you to look me straight in the eye when you answer it."

Michael rose to his feet, a lightning storm slowly building up behind his hooded eyes. Valenti stood his ground, his posture relaxed, an island of calm. Liz looked on anxiously. Maria worried that Michael was about to make his problems a whole lot worse.

But when Michael spoke, his tone was surprisingly placid. "I know what you're going to ask. So ask."

"All right, Michael. Did you kill Hank Whitmore?"

Michael met Valenti's gaze without flinching. "No. Satisfied?"

"As a matter of fact . . . *yes*," Valenti said, evidently taking Michael's statement completely at face value. Maria was impressed, though she still feared that Michael might fly off the handle just because Valenti had dared to ask the question.

But Michael's anger already seemed to have fizzled, replaced by something that Maria interpreted as a mixture of surprise and gratitude.

"Thanks," he said, his voice barely above a whisper. Maria thought he might cry.

She walked over to Michael and put her arms around him. "Thank *you*," she said.

"For what?" he said, pulling away from her slightly to look her in the eye.

"For not, you know, zapping your benefactor."

Michael looked disappointed. "You really thought I'd do that?"

"I thought you might," Maria said, mock-seriously. "Whether you really meant to or not. I don't know if I've ever mentioned this to you before, but you do have a bit of a temper. It's a maturity thing."

"Well, I guess life in the Big House makes you grow up fast," Michael said with a small, sidewise smile.

Valenti cleared his throat. "All right then, now that the main issue is settled, let's talk specifically about what we're going to say in Judge Lewis's chambers tomorrow." Valenti focused on Michael. "I think we ought to start with when you last saw Hank Whitmore."

Michael nodded. "I never saw him again after the night I finally left the old drunk's trailer."

"Can anybody vouch for that?"

"Max and Liz can. They came to the trailer and saw the old man blow his top. But they also saw me use my powers to stop him from ventilating us with a shotgun."

"Hmmm. I thought for a moment it would be a good idea to get Max and Isabel to testify at the hearing. But maybe it's a good thing that they went out of town with Kyle instead."

Liz looked quizzical. "Why's that?"

"There's too much they'd have to hold back. We have to give Judge Lewis clear-cut answers that he can accept, not more questions. And that's going to be hard enough to do, given Lewis's attitude toward me—and given that I'm going to be testifying tomorrow."

Maria shook her head, confused. "If Lewis really does have it in for you, then why risk ticking him off anymore by testifying?"

Valenti gave her a wan smile. "Because I'm Michael's best alibi."

"Not true," Maria said. "Michael spent the entire night with me after he left Whitmore's trailer. And Mom saw us both the next morning, in my bedroom. I'll swear to that right in front of God, the president, and Judge Lewis."

Valenti shook his head. "Now that would just thrill your mother all to pieces, wouldn't it? No, I don't want you or your mother dragged any further into this. The stuff that helps the most has to come from me, since I was the last one to see Whitmore before he left town."

"Maybe you did," Michael said. "Maybe you didn't."

Valenti scowled. "What do you mean?"

"I mean that the man you saw might not have been Whitmore at all. What if it was really Nasedo? He was a shape-shifter, after all. What if he'd already killed Hank, then tried to cover it up by letting you think you'd seen him alive afterward?"

"I've suspected Nasedo's involvement ever since Hanson's people uncovered the body," Valenti said, nodding.

"If I could get a look at the body myself," Liz said, "it might help us shed some light on that."

Maria shook her head. "Good plan, Agent Scully.

Maybe you should sneak in and perform an autopsy of your own. Then when Hanson catches you at it, he'll conveniently forget all about railroading Michael. Keen."

Valenti chuckled. Looking at a scowling Liz, he said, "Maria's right. Let's solve one problem before we risk creating another. Besides, I got a pretty close look at Whitmore's remains. It's obvious from the hand-shaped hole burned into his chest that alien powers of some sort were what did him in. And I don't think even you have a way to dust for Nasedo's fingerprints, Liz. No offense."

"Fine," Liz said, sounding glum. "I withdraw the suggestion."

Maria felt a pang of sympathy for her friend. *She just wants to help out and keep busy—at least until she can have her showdown with Max.*

The front door suddenly opened. Amy DeLuca strode into the living room, looking tired after a long shift at the shop. "Goddess, what a terrible day I had. The liquid incense spilled all over the—"

She jerked to a halt, an eager smile jolting the fatigue from her face. "Jim! What a surprise!"

Judging from Valenti's reaction, Maria imagined that his picture must be printed in the dictionary right next to the word *awkward*. For the past year and a half or so she'd been aware—sometimes uncomfortably—of her mom's on-again/off-again relationship with Valenti.

"Just, ah, chatting with the kids, Amy," Valenti stammered. "And waiting for you." He crossed to Amy and gave her a chaste kiss on the forehead. Amy beamed and brushed Valenti's hand with her fingertips.

Maria's nose wrinkled involuntarily. Addressing Liz and

Michael, she said, "Okay. That's our cue to get out of here. Shall we repair to the Crashdown, where no one indulges in blatant and excessive displays of physical affection?"

Michael and Liz both made noises of agreement, then trooped toward the door. Maria cast a parting glance over her shoulder as she followed her friends out to the Jetta.

"Don't do anything I wouldn—"

"Good-*bye,* Maria," Amy said. She and Valenti stood looking silently at each other, hands at their sides, their faces both as red as cured hams.

I don't wanna even think about it, Maria thought as she got in the car.

Sitting in an unmarked car across the street and three houses away from the DeLuca home, Deputy Owen Blackwood felt a sense of relief that night had finally fallen. Under the cover of darkness, his dirty deeds would be much better concealed.

When Hanson had ordered him to keep Valenti under surveillance—in the hopes of finding him meeting secretly with Michael Guerin and company—Blackwood had protested invading his former boss's privacy. But Randy, always the stubborn taskmaster, had insisted.

So here I am, Blackwood thought ruefully, chewing the last remnants of a greasy drive-through hamburger. *Skulking in the shadows.*

Blackwood had no doubt that Valenti had spotted the tail immediately. He probably knew exactly who was following him, and why, and was obviously smart enough not to let on that he knew. Jim Valenti was just too experienced in the lawman's craft to be caught unawares like that.

Sure do miss the guy. When those city council paper pushers tossed him, Roswell lost the finest damned sheriff it ever had.

Crumpling an assortment of wrappers and napkins into a grease-spattered paper bag, Blackwood saw a sudden flash of motion on the driveway in front of the DeLuca house. Three teenagers got into a beat-up Jetta and drove away. Blackwood noted that the group had consisted of Michael Guerin, Liz Parker, and Maria DeLuca, the daughter of the owner of record for the car, as he'd learned a few minutes earlier when he'd run the license plates through the mobile computer.

But there was no sign of Valenti. His truck was still parked at the curbside, near a second vehicle the computer had said was owned by one Amy DeLuca, Maria's mother.

Jim's still inside. Trying to live his life in peace.

But Blackwood had his orders. He picked up the squawk box and thumbed the button. "Sheriff Hanson, this is Deputy Blackwood."

"Hanson here. Report, Deputy."

Why can't he just call me "Owen," the way Jim always did?

Heaving a great sigh of resignation, Blackwood went into the terse "Joe Friday" mode that Hanson seemed to like so much. "Jim Valenti is still inside the DeLuca house, Sheriff, with Maria DeLuca's mother, one Amy DuLuca. I just observed Mr. Guerin leaving the premises, along with Maria DeLuca and Elizabeth Parker."

Despite his affection for Valenti, even Blackwood had to admit that meeting with Michael Guerin barely an hour after Hanson had reluctantly released him from jail looked a little fishy.

"Good work, Deputy."

Blackwood was getting fidgety, and wasn't feeling terribly good about himself. He failed to keep the acid from his stomach entirely out of his voice when he replied, "Thanks, Fearless Leader. Who do you want me to spy on next?"

Unsurprisingly, Hanson seemed oblivious. "Get back to the station, Deputy Blackwood."

Starting the car, Blackwood said, "Ten-four, Chief. Then what?"

There was a brief crackle of static as Blackwood drove off. "Then, nothing," Hanson said. "I think I'm gonna have to bring in some bigger guns to find out what's really going on between Jim Valenti and those kids."

12

Zan could feel the electricity in the air as the *kesters* glided over the sea. The cool blue water reached toward the horizon, reflecting the trio of moons which had just begun to rise.

He looked down the beach and saw three people—two women and a man—disrobing at the water's edge. One of the women splashed into the water first, but it rolled in heavier waves, not giving the salty spray he remembered from . . . where *was* it he remembered it from?

Few people knew of his retreat here, and he preferred to keep it that way. His duties kept him busy enough that he almost never had time to himself. Enjoying an evening of peace and solitude under the moonlight would allow him to better deal with the building conflict among the system's faction leaders. Tomorrow would be a decisive day, not only for Antar, but for all five of the worlds under his rule.

He chewed a piece of *roral* grass as he watched the trio of lovers frolic in the surf. They had to be a unit; their attentions and affections toward one another were too familiar to imply otherwise. It made him smile. He and Ava had been like that once, before the crushing weight of his duties began to wear at their relationship, just as it wore at his energy . . . and recently, his soul.

He stood and removed his shirt, his long hair ruffling in the wind. The cool breeze played on his skin, and the energy from his body gave it a slight glow. *The water looks inviting,* he thought. *I have time for a brief swim before I have to be back.*

Pain suddenly lanced into him from behind, and Zan felt himself teetering. He fell forward, onto his hands and knees, barely able to keep his weight from crashing off the ledge and tumbling down the rocks to the sea. As he turned, he put a hand up to his chest, where something wet was dripping.

Behind him, standing in the shadows of the cave entrance that led to his secret retreat, were two figures. One of them stepped out of the shadows, and he saw his attacker. Kivar stooped and grabbed Zan's discarded shirt, using it to wipe the king's blood off the weapon in his hands.

Zan tried to say something, but no sound would leave his mouth. He removed his hand from his chest and saw blood on it. His blood. He reached for Kivar, even as the other figure stepped out of the darkness. It was a woman, but her face was shifting and indistinct. It was his sister Vilandra one moment, his wife Ava the next, and then an almond-eyed, black-haired girl with silver antennae bobbing from atop her head.

From underneath the cloak of the woman emerged a

blue gelatinous liquid, and even as it poured across the ground, coming toward him as if with a purpose, it began to form the shape of an infant. The babe crawled toward him, its head overly large, its large oval eyes black as midnight pools. He could see his own face reflected in those eyes, shock, terror, and wonder all etched in his features.

Wordlessly, Kivar stepped over to Zan, Kivar's cloak sweeping over the baby, and he bent down. One strong hand, its fingers greenish and overly long, gripped Zan's neck, and he felt himself being lifted off the ground. He stared into the eyes of his assailant, and was astonished to see Kivar's features change as well. He was no longer Kivar, but Rath, then no longer Rath, but an older man, creases lining his face, then no longer the man but a boy, his dark hair short, his ears protruding on either side of his head.

And then the Kivar/Rath/Man/Boy pushed him backward, and Zan could feel the electricity in the air again, could see the moons above him as he tumbled downward. His entry into the ocean was not painful. Indeed, the water received him like a lover, embracing him. The thickness of the sea surrounded him, encased him. He used all his strength to push at it, dimly aware of a need to break the surface, to find another ship, to get his son back from Tess, to let Liz know how much he loved her. . . .

His strength was almost gone, but it was enough to bring him to the surface. He couldn't see the cliff outcropping from which he had been thrown, but a red light that spelled out the word VACANCY with neon tubes flashed at him, winking as if to taunt the dying king.

Arms enfolded him from below, and he struggled against them. The water churned, and in the luminescence he saw a girl with short hair the color of sand. He somehow knew she was Tess, and he tried to scream her name, but as the air escaped his mouth in bubbles, the scream that came out was, "Ava!"

Her hands clutched him again, pulling him down, shaking him, and he lashed out, seeing Tess, seeing Vilandra, seeing a baby with dark eyes, seeing three pale silver moons in an orange sky. . . .

"Maxwell! Stop it!" The sharp voice caught him, and he awoke with a start. Groggily, Max realized he was in his car, sleeping stretched out in the backseat, a light jacket thrown over his face. He shook his head to focus, and saw Kyle on the driver's side and Isabel on the passenger's side, both staring over the seat at him, concern evident on their faces. Behind them, out the window, he saw a hotel sign for the Silver Trio Inn, a red neon vacancy sign blinking below it.

"Damn, man! What were you dreaming about?" Kyle asked.

"Sorry," Max muttered, rubbing a hand over his face. "Did I . . . was I . . ."

"You were talking in what I'm guessing is *Antarian*," Isabel said. "I recognized some of the names. *Our* names."

Max sat up, still groggy. "Yeah. Weird dream. It was like pieces of my alien memories mixed in with parts of my life now." He looked to either side of the car. "Are we there yet?"

"We're at the outskirts of Santa Fe," Kyle said. "I figured this is where we'd find the cheaper motels."

"What time is it?"

"Almost one A.M.," Isabel answered. "We've been

driving—Kyle's been driving—for the last four hours, since we took that last rest stop break."

"Wow, I must have really been out of it," Max said, rubbing his eyes.

"You were fine until about ten minutes ago," Isabel said. "And then you started speaking in tongues and thrashing around."

"Sorry," Max said sheepishly.

"I'm gonna go in and get us a room," Kyle said. "You stay out here, Max. You look terrible."

"I'll come with you," Isabel said. Kyle nodded.

As they walked away from the car toward the motel office, Max struggled to grasp at the remains of his dream. Already it had whispered its way out of his mind, tucking back into his subconscious memories. He couldn't recall any specifics other than a beach, but he knew his chest hurt. *Must have been the burrito I had the last time we stopped.* The sugar substitute he had sprinkled on it always gave him heartburn.

Isabel took the lead as they went into the hotel office. Behind the desk was a fortyish man with a thick, graying mustache and several discreet piercings in his ears. "Good evening," he offered. "May I help you?"

"We'd like a room, please," Isabel said, flashing him a killer smile and tossing her hair back over her shoulder with a roll of her head.

It didn't have any effect on the man. He looked over at Kyle for a moment, then back to her. "There's a convention in town, so all the hotels are pretty much all full up. All *we* have left is a room with two single beds. Is that all right?"

"Sure, Kyle will be sleeping with my brother, and I'll take the second bed."

The man visibly brightened, then grinned over at Kyle. "Well, in that case, I'll give you a little *extra* discount on the rate. I like to take care of 'family.'"

Isabel was momentarily confused, then realized what the desk clerk was saying. "Thank you. That's so *sweet*."

She put the room on her credit card, and got the keys. Handing one to Kyle, she opened the door for him and turned to the clerk. "Thanks again."

"Thank you, Ms. Evans. Have a good night," the man called to Kyle.

On their way back to the car, Isabel could no longer stifle her giggles. Kyle stopped, and looked at her. "What's so funny? And what was all that 'family' stuff about?"

"He thought you were *gay*," she said, laughing.

Kyle was surprised. "*What*? Why?"

"Probably because I said you were sleeping with Max." She laughed again, then added, "The reference to 'family' was kind of a code word for 'one of us.' He was gay, too."

"Hmmm," Kyle said. "Well, I hope at least he thought I was cute."

Isabel's eyes widened. "Well, Mr. Valenti, how *progressive* of you."

He moved over to the driver's side of the car, looking relieved that Max wasn't asleep again in the backseat. "Contrary to popular opinion, not all ex-football jocks are homophobes. Some of us—especially those of us who practice Buddhism—might even be a little *enlightened* as to the diversity present in the world."

He opened the door for her, then added one more

thought. "After all, if I can handle driving around with aliens, I think I can be pretty comfortable with humans of all kinds."

Isabel was aware her mouth was hanging slightly open, and she closed it with a snap as she got into the car. *Maybe Kyle isn't quite the simple bo-hunk he always appears to be.*

As soon as they got into the room and dropped off their bags, Kyle announced that he was going to get some snacks from the vending machine. Isabel waited until he was out of the room, then turned to Max pointedly. "What *exactly* was going on in your dream? You said all of our alien names several times."

Max sat down on the edge of the bed, scowling a bit at the too-busy green ivy print on the bedspread. "I don't remember. It went out of my head almost the moment I woke up. I think I was dreaming about home—"

"You mean Antar," Isabel said, interrupting. "*Earth* is our home."

Max sighed heavily. "Yes, I mean Antar. Look, I don't want to get into semantic quibbles right now, Iz. I'm too tired."

She decided to let it go and headed toward the bathroom, carrying her hastily packed amenities bag.

Max called after her. "You said earlier you were supposed to have dinner with somebody tonight. Anybody I know?"

"None of your business, Max," she said, peering around the door. She saw that Kyle had just walked in.

"Oooh, that must mean it's serious," Kyle said, throwing a bag of chips and several candy bars down on the tabletop.

Deciding to let that comment go by, Isabel closed the bathroom door. Leaning over the sink, she splashed some water on her face, then looked at her reflection in the mirror. It had jarred her to hear Max say the name Vilandra while he was dreaming. She still wasn't sure what role she had played during her past on Antar. *Was I the loving sister and faithful princess, or did I bring about the downfall of my brother's reign?*

Of all of the "Royal Four," Isabel seemed to connect to her homeworld the least; unlike Max and Liz, and Maria and Michael, she had never let anyone into her soul, so she hadn't shared flashes of her past with anyone—and thus knew virtually nothing about her previous life on Antar. She supposed she could have tried some kind of memory-jogging mind-meld thing with Tess, given that they both had more highly developed pseudo-psychic abilities than the boys, but in retrospect she was glad she hadn't.

Maybe Jesse will be the one who I share those visions with someday. Maybe he's my soul mate. The thought made her smile. Then the demon of doubt entered her mind, unbidden. *Of course, that would mean I'd have to tell him the truth. And I don't know that Max or Michael would go for that. Or if Jesse would, for that matter.*

She exited the bathroom and saw Max and Kyle sitting on the bed, noshing on candy bars and flipping through TV channels with the remote.

"Anything good on?" she asked.

"No porn," Kyle said with a slight frown. "But *Independence Day* is on Showtime, and *Mars Attacks!* is on HBO." The frown changed to a smirk.

So much for my impression that Kyle had evolved. She gave him a pained smile, then grabbed the remote from him, clicking the TV off. "I think we'll leave the alien invasions alone for a while. Besides, we need to get some sleep so we can get into the university early in the morning. We don't know what Skarrstin's office hours are."

Kyle turned to Max, but pointed at Isabel. "Is she always this much of a killjoy?"

"Yup," Max said.

Isabel glared at Max as she kicked off her shoes, then set the alarm clock and shut off the overhead light. "Seven o'clock is going to come early, boys," she said with impish glee.

She climbed under the covers, turning her back to the boys. Behind her, she heard Kyle sigh heavily and gather up his candy wrappers. "If Max goes into another one of his alien nightmares, I'm getting into bed with you, Isabel."

Max laughed. Isabel didn't even turn over to respond. "If you climb into bed with me, Kyle, you'll be in an alien nightmare of your own."

With that, Isabel tuned out the sounds in the room and willed herself into her own personal world of dreams. She hoped Jesse would be there to greet her.

13

Valenti awoke to the sound of an insistently ringing telephone. Squinting in the midmorning sunlight, he rolled out of bed and searched for several moments through the clutter of laundry. He glanced at the clock radio on the bedside table. Seven fifty-seven.

"Valenti here," he said into the cordless handset.

"Hope I'm not disturbing you, Jim," said a familiar voice on the other end of the phone. The voice belonged to Sheriff Hanson. Hanson's friendly tone made Valenti wonder whether the young sheriff was feeling guilty about the aspersions he'd cast his way at the sheriff's station the previous day.

"Morning, Randy," Valenti said. "This must be the first time we've spoken two days in a row since I was your boss. I hope you don't need another corpse identified."

"No, it's nothing like that, Jim," Hanson said after a brief pause. "But you'd still better come over to the station now just the same. And be prepared to answer a few hard questions."

Valenti scowled. Something was wrong. "What's this about?" he said, though he felt sure it had to involve their conversation the previous day about Michael Guerin.

"Let's just say there's somebody here who expects to see you right away," Hanson said. "Somebody a lot more important than me." It was becoming clear to the ex-sheriff that this was all he was going to learn—at least until he made yet another in-person visit to his old office at central Roswell's sheriff station.

Valenti was already eyeing the heaps of laundry that were scattered across the bedroom, seeking something to wear that might make him look presentable. Though he missed wearing the khaki uniform, he had found it surprisingly easy these past few months to adjust to puttering in his wood shop, where he wore mostly T-shirts and sweatpants.

God, but how this place has deteriorated since Tess left. Left to their own devices, Valenti and his son Kyle tended to live like a couple of undergrads in some low-rent fraternity house. *I've got to get Kyle to help me clean some of this mess up.*

"Jim?" Hanson said. Valenti realized then that he must have lapsed into woolgathering. He was doing that entirely too much these days.

"I'll be right over," he said before ringing off.

Valenti's drive to the sheriff's station took maybe ten minutes. After passing through the reception area, Valenti found the sheriff standing alone in his outer office.

Something was clearly wrong. "Mind telling me what this is all about, Randy?" Valenti asked.

Looking uncomfortable, Hanson gestured toward his inner office door. "I think it'd be best if we discuss things in private."

Valenti didn't like this one bit. Glancing at his watch, he saw that he had barely an hour left until his meeting with Michael and the other kids. Sighing in irritation, he walked to the familiar door, pushing it open. He wished the new sheriff would stop beating around the bush and would simply tell him who was waiting to speak with him—and what it was all about.

Valenti stepped into the spartan office, with the sheriff following immediately behind him. And Valenti suddenly had a pretty good idea what was to be discussed.

"Dan," Valenti said, nodding toward the mustached, middle-aged man who was sitting behind the sheriff's desk. "You look a year younger every time I see you. What brings the State Police Board to my former office this fine morning?"

Dan Lubetkin looked up from the file he had been reading. Valenti noted that his old friend's navy suit coat looked rumpled, as though he'd been up all night fretting over a case.

Fretting over me, Valenti thought, seeing his own name on the manila folder in Lubetkin's hands. He carefully arranged his poker face, resolving to give away nothing he didn't have to. He thought of the three kids who depended on him even now to keep the wolves away from their doors.

"Please have a seat, Jim," Lubetkin said, pointing toward a chair on the other side of the desk. The man's face was a dispassionate mask. Although Valenti had considered Dan a friend for many years before the alien teens had come into his life, it was clear that Lubetkin had come in an entirely professional capacity. Old loyalties weren't going to cut him much slack today.

And Valenti was growing steadily more rankled by mounting tension he sensed in both Hanson and Lubetkin, as well as by their lack of directness. He folded his arms and leaned against a file cabinet instead of taking the proffered chair.

"So tell me why you've come all the way down from Albuquerque today, Dan," Valenti said simply.

Lubetkin scowled from behind the desk, and Hanson closed the door behind him. "Sit down, Jim," the sheriff said, gesturing toward the chair.

Nodding silently to his former protégé, Valenti sat. Glowering at Lubetkin, he leaned forward over his side of the desk, planting an elbow on the wood with a solid *thunk*. "All right, Dan. I'm here, and you have my full attention. *And* a complete file on me."

Lubetkin only stared at him in silence for a protracted moment. Finally, he said, "It's hard to know exactly where to start, Jim."

Valenti smiled. "The beginning is usually a good place."

"All right," Lubetkin said, nodding. "Maybe you're right. The beginning, then." He opened the manila folder and placed it on the desk in front of Valenti.

Valenti looked down and saw a glossy black-and-white photograph of a dead man who appeared to be approximately sixty years of age. He was shirtless, lying on a pathologist's slab, a small bullet-entry wound visible on his chest. Valenti did his best to conceal the upwelling of sadness and rage that the image evoked.

"Do you recognize the man in this photograph, Jim?"

Even in death, the man's face was one Valenti knew he could never forget. "Everett Hubble," he said. "A man obsessed with tracking down his wife's killer. And who thought his wife had died at the hands of some sort of . . . space alien."

Valenti knew that the person Hubble had sought was indeed an alien, a shape-shifting humanoid who had some truly remarkable, unearthly powers. And he was also bitterly aware that Hubble's alien-hunting fixation had also helped end his father's career as Roswell's sheriff.

"And Hubble is also a man you shot to death," Lubetkin said.

"That's right. You've read my report. It's all on the official record."

Lubetkin raised an eyebrow significantly as he reached for the photograph, returned it to the folder, and dropped the whole thing on his side of the desk. "Is it, Jim?"

Valenti tried to keep a lid on his temper, but could feel himself building toward a slow boil nevertheless. "Damn it, Dan, I thought we went over this the last time you came to Roswell. Why rehash this business again now?"

Lubetkin closed his eyes and pinched the bridge of his nose, giving the appearance of a man whose job had been making him extraordinarily tired of late.

"All right, Jim," Lubetkin said a moment later, locking his gaze firmly with Valenti's. "Hubble's death is just one piece in a larger pattern of . . . insufficiently explained behavior on your part. Like the miraculous way you figured out precisely where the kidnapped Dupree girl was being held captive last year. Not to mention the fact that mysteriously irradiated human remains have turned up twice around Roswell in as many years—with you and those teenage kids just happening to be at least peripherally connected to both incidents."

Valenti swallowed, but otherwise kept his face impassive. "I filed full reports on each and every one of those incidents."

"Yes, you have," Lubetkin said. "And I've read them all, as has your former deputy." He nodded to Hanson, who shifted from one foot to the other, obviously not enjoying the sight of his former boss being grilled.

Continuing to look Valenti straight in the eye, Lubetkin continued. "In fact, I've read each of your reports repeatedly. Every 'I' is dotted and every 't' is crossed. So why is it that after months of careful study, I'm still convinced you're holding back something significant?"

Valenti slowly rose to his feet and allowed a humorless smile to stretch his face taut. "You tell me, Dan. Maybe you're just suspicious by nature."

"Or maybe you have a reason to deliberately mislead everyone, Jim. A reason you're not comfortable being candid about."

"Is there a point to this inquisition?" Valenti said, willing his hands not to clench into fists. It almost worked.

"All right. Let me come right out with it."

"I was starting to think that you Internal Affairs types weren't capable of that."

Lubetkin ignored the jab. "What's your relationship with those kids, Jim? And don't give me that innocent 'what kids?' look. You know damned well who I'm talking about—Max and Isabel Evans, Michael Guerin, and the

Harding girl you had living in your home for a while last year."

Valenti took a deep breath before responding. "I think you're overstepping your authority here, Dan. In case you haven't been keeping up with current events, I don't work as a law enforcement officer these days. So my personal life is none of your business."

"You know better than that, Jim," Hanson said, steel in his voice though he looked heartsick. "When the safety of the people of Roswell might be at stake, *anybody's* personal life is fair game. Or is Mr. Lubetkin right? *Are* you hiding something?"

Valenti searched both men's faces for a way out, but found none. He was going to have to tell them *something*. With a sigh, he plopped himself back into the chair.

"You know that my seventeen-year-old son lives with me," Valenti said. "He's a sociable boy who has plenty of friends."

Lubetkin nodded. "Yes. Kyle. He's also something of an athlete, I understand."

"He lettered in football, wrestling, and cross-country," Valenti confirmed, nodding. "I've devoted myself to raising him and I give him every bit of encouragement and help that I can."

Lubetkin frowned impatiently. "We all know what a dedicated father you are."

"Then it might interest you to know that not all of Kyle's classmates are as fortunate as he is in that regard. Some teenagers don't have father figures they can rely on."

"You're talking about Michael Guerin," Hanson said.

"He's a good case in point," Valenti said.

"Guerin," Lubetkin repeated, a thoughtful expression crossing his features. "I've read his file too. Now there's a kid desperately in need of a wholesome father figure if I ever saw one."

"My point exactly."

"So why does your path keep crossing with the Evans kids as well? They're anything but homeless, antisocial street urchins."

"No," Valenti said, desperately searching for an appropriate response. "But they *are* orphans." He instantly regretted having pointed this out; the last thing he wanted was to cause Lubetkin to scrutinize the strange origins of Max and Isabel, who with Michael were placed in an orphanage after they had been found wandering naked in the desert as small children. Of course, Max and Isabel hadn't stayed in the orphanage for long; Phillip and Diane Evans had adopted them quickly. Very few people besides Valenti himself knew that these children had literally "hatched" from alien gestation chambers shortly before their discovery by the state child welfare authorities.

"Max and Isabel were adopted about a decade ago," Lubetkin said, "into a quite well-to-do family, it seems. Phillip Evans is a practicing attorney, after all. The Evans kids are anything but deprived. Something doesn't quite add up here."

"Phillip Evans is a busy man," Valenti said, thinking quickly. "There's plenty of room in Max's and Isabel's lives for some friendship and mentoring. The same sort of guidance I've always given to Kyle."

"Ah. Mentoring and guidance. Perhaps that explains

why you took in the daughter of Ed Harding, the military contractor, after his death last year."

"Tess was another one of Kyle's friends," Valenti said. "Friends help one another."

"Indeed they do. But why is it I still can't shake the feeling that there's something more going on between you and these kids? Let me cut right to the point, Jim. You suddenly went from obsessively chasing signs of aliens—a hobby that seems a good deal more harmless with you than it was with your father, except in Mr. Hubble's case—to mentoring a quartet of teens and their assorted hangers-on. Now what exactly is going on?"

Lubetkin's tone was getting more hostile, and Valenti was finding it increasingly difficult to rein in his anger.

"If you're going to accuse me of something, Dan, then I suggest you get it right out into the open. And if you've really read my reports as carefully as you say you have, then you know I'm not very patient with innuendo and rumormongering." Valenti stood again and walked toward the door.

Seeming to understand that he'd gone too far, Lubetkin rose and held up a hand in a placating gesture. "All right, Jim. We'll leave all that aside for now. But there's still one more very important thing that we have to discuss."

Valenti paused, his hand on the door. Turning back to face Dan and the sheriff, he said, "And what's that?"

"There's still the little matter of what's going on with Michael Guerin. And whether or not he's capable of murder."

Valenti remained firmly convinced of Michael's innocence. His prime suspect was still the late shape-changer

Nasedo, who had, like Valenti, also acted as a mentor and protector to Roswell's half-alien teens.

What Valenti still *couldn't* do was explain any of this— not without placing Max, Isabel, and Michael in even greater danger of having their extraterrestrial origins exposed.

"Michael's the entire point of all of this, isn't he?" said Valenti.

"You've been seen in his company since the remains of Mr. Guerin's foster father turned up on the outskirts of town yesterday. And you've met with the Evans kids as well."

Valenti wasn't surprised to learn that he'd been spied upon. "Is chatting with my son's teenage friends suddenly a crime?"

Hanson fidgeted, apparently also growing impatient with Lubetkin's roundabout interrogation. "Of course it's not, Jim. But withholding information relevant to a murder investigation is a whole different kettle of fish."

"So you think I know something that connects Michael to Whitmore's murder," Valenti said.

Hanson nodded. "It's no secret that Hank Whitmore used to beat the kid up from time to time. As well as his various wives."

Valenti's response was tart. "Didn't we cover this ground yesterday? I feel like I'm trapped in a CD that just keeps playing the same damned song. Of *course* it's no secret. That's why Michael got himself legally emancipated as soon as Whitmore staggered out of his life. But if you really had any solid evidence on Michael, you wouldn't have had to release him before his hearing."

"True enough," Lubetkin said, sitting on the edge of Hanson's desk. "Perhaps you've laid my suspicions about Mr. Guerin to rest. Maybe he really *is* no killer."

"Of course he's no killer," Valenti said.

"But *somebody* is," Lubetkin said, raising his voice slightly. "Jim, you say that Mr. Guerin and these other teens look to you as a mentor and father figure."

Valenti felt he was being maneuvered by a clever lawyer. "I try. You'd have to ask *them* how they view me. What are you driving at now?"

"Just this: You knew about Whitmore's tendency toward domestic violence. In fact, you had arrested him a number of times—once you even broke his arm while doing so. As Mr. Guerin's surrogate father and protector, you must have been tempted to intervene on the kid's behalf—maybe even with lethal force."

Valenti felt as though he'd been gut-punched. He'd been expecting to have to continue to vouch for Michael. But Valenti hadn't expected to stand accused of Whitmore's murder himself.

"You'd better be prepared to back that up, Dan," Valenti said, his voice low and dangerous. He could barely restrain an impulse to leap across the desk at his old friend. Lubetkin, however, was merely studying him, wearing a neutral expression. He was obviously fishing for an unguarded, incriminating emotional reaction.

Valenti carefully blanked his face, determined not to give him the satisfaction of seeing *any* of his reactions.

But Lubetkin had obviously sensed Valenti's outrage. "Oh, there's no need to get self-righteous, Jim," the mustached man said. "Remember, there are still a lot of incidents from your recent past you've never explained to my satisfaction, official reports or no. Like the harassment lawsuit the geologist Grant Sorenson had filed against you. Then there's the Laurie Dupree and Everett Hubble incidents. Also, let's not forget your confusing account of the Liz Parker shooting incident two years ago. And don't get me started on the little misunderstanding you caused at the UFO Center last month. Sheriff Hanson tells me that he called in sharpshooters from the State Police because *you* led him to believe that an armed gunman had taken hostages there."

Hanson coughed into his hand, looking nervous.

Valenti had finally heard enough. "Everything you need to know is covered in my official reports and statements," he said, pushing the door open. He stopped to glare quickly at both Lubetkin and Hanson. "So unless you're planning on either putting me back on the payroll or arresting me, that's where things are going to stand."

Fuming, he walked quickly out of Hanson's office. He didn't bother to watch either man's reaction.

14

UNIVERSITY OF SANTA FE

Dr. Jolene Skarrstin allowed herself to daydream for a moment as she walked down the corridor. In her mind's eye, she visualized herself standing on a stage before a distinguished audience of academics. Rows and rows of her fellow scientists and researchers applauded appreciatively, until the selection committee chairman signaled for silence.

It was time for her to speak.

Cradled in her sweaty hands was the cool metal medallion the Nobel Prize committee had just presented to her. Bedecked in a splendid blue gown, she squared her strong shoulders, held her head high, and addressed her assembled colleagues.

I'd like to thank the selection committee for recognizing my humble efforts to control humanity's genetic afflictions, she said, *through the study of, ah, oozing blue space-goo.*

The ineptitude of her dream-speech shocked Dr.

Skarrstin back to reality as she rounded a corner and approached the door to her office. The imaginary Nobel medal abruptly vanished from her hands, replaced by the grim reality of a lipstick-smeared Styrofoam coffee cup, whose contents was neither hot enough nor brown enough to suit her. She came to a stop in front of her office door and took a swallow.

Fortunately, Skarrstin's office hours weren't due to begin for another hour, so she anticipated few distractions while she transcribed the previous day's research notes. Once that task was behind her, she felt she'd be able to give her graduate biochemistry students her full attention. Even after nearly twenty years as a member of the university's faculty, she still found influencing the minds and attitudes of young people to be a rewarding experience—in spite of the lousy coffee. There were times, though—not often—when she wondered whether providing guidance to these kids was satisfying mainly because she had never had children of her own.

Anticipating a stimulating afternoon's work, Jolene fumbled in her jacket pocket for the keys to her office— and heard voices, coming from just beyond the door. Frowning, she grasped the knob and turned it.

The door wasn't locked. The hairs on her neck stood on end.

Peeking around the door, Skarrstin heaved a sigh of relief. Seated behind the desk was Joyce Markowicz, one of her research assistants, and one of the very select handful of people she had entrusted with the keys to her office. In front of the desk stood a trio of teenagers, two boys and a girl, their backs to her.

Evidently deep in conversation with her three visitors, Joyce took a moment to look up and acknowledge Skarrstin's entry. Smiling, the assistant said, "Oh, Dr. Skarrstin. Let me introduce you to some youngsters who are very curious about biochemistry. They've come all the way from Roswell to ask you a few scientific questions."

Skarrstin smiled and took another sip of her coffee. "Roswell? My, to come this far, you three must be prospective undergrads. Hello. I'm Jolene Skarrstin."

As she began to speak, the teens turned away from Joyce and faced Skarrstin. The nearest of the three, a strapping lad with tousled brown hair, smiled and extended a hand, which she shook. "Glad to meet you, Dr. Skarrstin. My name's Kyle Valenti."

Out of very long habit, she ran his face through her mental inventory of people she had met throughout her life. She quickly concluded that she had never seen him before.

"Good to meet you, Kyle," she said, returning his smile.

Nodding toward his companions, Kyle said, "And these are my friends, Max and Isabel Evans."

Skarrstin turned her gaze to the other two teens, a dark-haired, brooding boy of perhaps seventeen, and an attractive, statuesque blond girl of approximately the same age. Again, she instinctively compared their faces to those stored in her decades-long archives of memories.

And found them.

"My God," Skarrstin said, her mouth falling open.

She had seen these two teens before, many decades ago, and under very different circumstances. *It's not possible,* she thought. *There's just no way this can be possible.*

But she couldn't doubt the evidence of her own eyes. Darryl and Christine were standing before her, every bit as real and as solid as they had been the last time she'd seen them. Not only had they *not* aged, they actually appeared to be a bit younger than they had when she'd first met them, more than half a century past.

Out of the corner of her eye, Skarrstin noticed that Joyce had come up beside her, a look of concern etched across her sun-cured features. "Dr. Skarrstin, are you all right?"

The universe seemed to collapse around Skarrstin, until it held nothing at all except for the intense stare of the brooding boy, the haunting eyes of the tall, blond girl, and Skarrstin's own dream-like recollections of that fateful day, so many years ago.

"You can't be!" Skarrstin said, her voice an almost inarticulate shriek. The coffee cup slipped from her fingers, spilling its contents onto the carpet.

She ran from the office as though the Devil himself were chasing her.

During his few moments of eye contact with Dr. Skarrstin, Max felt a surge of recognition, a weird feeling of familiarity that seemed to burrow down to the core of his being. It went beyond the fact that she looked like Tess, grown older.

Then she was gone, running down the hallway. Max had never before seen anyone become so frightened so quickly. Perhaps she, too, had experienced that flash of recognition.

So why is she so terrified?

"I'm really sorry about this," the research assistant said, her face a road map of surprise. Jolene Skarrstin's panicked footfalls were still echoing down the hallway as she ran from the office. Max restrained an impulse to chase her, since that would seem suspicious. Maybe they could catch up to her later.

"Listen," the assistant was saying, speaking to all three of them at once, "I really should go after her and see if she's okay. Maybe we can schedule an appointment for you to see her some other time."

It was clear to Max that they had no choice but to follow the assistant as she shepherded them out into the hallway. He watched dispiritedly as the tanned young woman took a key out of her pocket and locked the door behind them.

I've got to get in there alone. Maybe Dr. Skarrstin has some files that might help us find our genetic templates. The fact that Skarrstin had seemed to recognize both him and Isabel made him hope that she had some firsthand knowledge of the original humans whose DNA had been used to create them.

Max turned toward Isabel. "Why don't you and Kyle help Joyce look for Dr. Skarrstin?"

Isabel nodded, while Kyle scowled. Max noted that Kyle never seemed pleased by abrupt changes to the existing plan.

"I'll wait around here, in case she comes back," Max added, for Kyle's benefit. Kyle finally seemed to understand that Max was really asking him to help lead the assistant away from the office.

"Thanks," the assistant said, nodding at Isabel. "I could

use the help. I'm not sure which way she went after she got around the corner."

A few moments later, the assistant, Isabel, and Kyle had scattered in different directions throughout the building, leaving Max standing alone before the locked door to Skarrstin's office.

After glancing down the hall in both directions to make certain no one was watching him, Max placed his right hand on the knob, closing his eyes to focus his power through his body and into the metal. His hand emitted a brief pulsation of light, and the knob suddenly turned in his hand. A moment later, he was in the office, closing the door behind him.

Max moved near the window, where he used his powers again to quickly unlock the drawers to a battered corner file cabinet. Inside were a collection of neatly organized manila folders, most of it concerning—not surprisingly—various aspects of biochemistry and genetics. He came across a draft of a scientific paper, authored by Skarrstin, titled "Oncological Applications of Therapeutic DNA Resequencing in Living Cells." There were charts, graphs, DNA profiles that appeared to belong to actual living people, records of experiments, catalogs of specimens—

Then something on the page almost leaped out at him. It was a photograph of a beaker filled with a gelatinous blue substance, along with some descriptive text. He quickly scanned a few paragraphs, confirming his initial impression. His heart raced.

Gandarium. She's working with the same blue ooze that tried to take over the world last year.

Another chart in the same folder showed what appeared to be electron microscope photographs of blood cells on a microscope slide. Cells which, like his own, appeared to be comprised of a fusion of human and alien organelles.

Max looked around the office for some means of copying the pictures and text he held in his hands. There wasn't time to sneak the stuff out of the office, copy it somewhere, and return it before anybody would miss it.

Then he spotted the small laptop computer that lay folded up on the desk amid several neat stacks of papers, sticky notes, and photographs. He felt for the small diskette in his jacket pocket.

I hope Dr. Skarrstin keeps her research on her hard drive.

Sitting behind the desk, Max opened the computer, turned it on, and set his hand on the screen, gently releasing some of his energy into the system as it booted up. A few moments later, he was past her security passwords. Slipping his diskette into the drive, he began searching through Skarrstin's labyrinth of cryptically named folders and files.

There was a tentative knock on the door, and a moment later it opened. Max began to breathe again when he saw Kyle's head duck inside the office. "Max!" he hissed.

"I think some of the information we need is on this computer," Max said.

Kyle peeked out into the hallway for a moment, then fixed his gaze back on Max. "There's no time!" he said in hushed tones. "I hear somebody coming."

Max quickly popped the diskette out and returned it to his pocket. He shut down the computer and closed it. He could hear the voices in the corridor, distant but quickly growing closer.

"Come on!" Kyle hissed impatiently. "We'll meet Isabel outside."

Max's eyes riffled the desktop one final time. He hesitated at one of the small piles of paper, which was topped by a dog-eared photograph. The picture showed Dr. Skarrstin standing on the banks of a river, surrounded by several young people who carried fishing equipment. Max figured them for some of her students. He stared into Skarrstin's eyes, the weird sensation of gut-level recognition returning.

"Let's *go!*" Kyle said, using a nails-on-a-chalkboard tone.

On impulse, Max snatched up the photograph and quickly followed Kyle out of the office.

"Where are we off to next?" Kyle said. He sat in the Chevy's backseat, a breeze gently brushing through his hair as Max pulled the car out of the university's main parking lot.

"Isn't it obvious?" Isabel said from the passenger seat. "Skarrstin's house. Since her assistant never located her, that's where we've got our best chance to find her."

"Oh," Kyle said. "Was her home address written down somewhere in her office?"

"Apparently not," Max said.

"So you got it off the Internet," Kyle said.

"Nope."

"Then you must have used your alien powers to track it down."

"Not this time."

Kyle frowned. "So you're just going to drive around and

use the Force until you find her place? *Good* plan. Very Zen. Why didn't *I* think of that?"

Isabel reached into her purse and dug out a torn and folded page of densely printed newsprint. "I used the Santa Fe White Pages. It's the next best thing to being there. Dr. Skarrstin's place isn't far from here."

"What else were you able to find in Skarrstin's office, Max?" Kyle wanted to know. "Besides her vacation photos, I mean."

"I didn't have enough time to make copies of any of it," Max said as he turned onto a major thoroughfare. "But what I saw told me that Dr. Skarrstin is definitely working on something that relates to the structure of hybrid DNA. And it involves the Gandarium."

"Gandarium. Yech," Isabel said, her nose wrinkling in distaste. Max supposed she was remembering how Grant Sorenson had kidnapped her while under the influence of the world-conquering blue viral ooze.

"I second that yech," Kyle said, mirroring Isabel's expression. "I was buried alive because of that stuff."

Max noted that Kyle had seemed none too thankful for being rescued in the nick of time that day. Of course, he knew that Kyle tended to blame him and his half-alien friends for virtually every weird incident that ever occurred in Roswell. *You're welcome,* Max thought, glancing at Kyle in the rearview mirror.

"Could she be working for the Skins?" Isabel said.

Max had already considered the possibility that Skarrstin was in league with the hide-shedding extraterrestrials they had tangled with last year. But something made him want to dismiss that notion out of hand. Perhaps it was the same impulse that convinced him that he was somehow personally connected to Jolene Skarrstin.

"I don't think so," Max said simply.

Kyle leaned forward, the wind whipping through his hair. "It doesn't have to be the Skins she's helping, you know. You Pod Squad types have no shortage of *other* enemies. And a lot of those come from your own homeworld. How do we know there aren't multiple alien races after you?"

"Don't remind me," Isabel said.

Max thought that Kyle had made a good point. Jolene Skarrstin definitely appeared to be the genetic template whose DNA had been used to create Tess. Even Kyle had commented on the resemblance. And Max still wondered if, like Tess, who had fled Earth with Max's unborn child, Skarrstin might also be planning to direct some act of treachery against the "Royal Four."

Make that "Royal Three," he thought. Thanks to Tess.

Max already knew something of Skarrstin's research. Now he had to understand her real intentions.

Following Isabel's directions, Max pulled into a parking lot that faced a large, stucco-covered apartment complex that resembled an ancient Anasazi pueblo. He stopped the car in an empty parking space in the lot's far corner, right beneath an air conditioner jutting from a second-floor window. Isabel and Kyle started to get out, but Max stopped them.

Reaching into the glove box, Max pulled out the photo of Skarrstin and her students that he had taken from the scientist's office. He handed the picture to Isabel.

"We have to know what her plans are, Isabel. Preferably

before we have another face-to-face encounter with her. Can you dreamwalk Skarrstin's photo? Sometimes you've been able to dreamwalk people who were awake. Do you think you can do it again now?"

Isabel stared at the image in her hand for a moment, then nodded. "I can give it a try."

She closed her eyes and began focusing her own unique power.

A swirl of light engulfed Isabel, then was gone as quickly as it had come. She was no longer sitting in Max's Chevy.

Opening her eyes, Isabel found herself standing in a hallway that vaguely resembled the corridors near Jolene Skarrstin's office. But this corridor seemed to stretch out into infinity in both directions. Along both sides of the hallway was a seemingly endless series of closed doors, each presumably leading to specific memories inside the mind of the person whose mind she was visiting.

In between the doors, the walls were covered with framed images—paintings and photographs. The images were coming in and out of focus, as though viewed through the lens of some mad photographer. Some of the likenesses were rendered with only a few broad brush-strokes, as though the artist who had created them had yet to finish them. It took Isabel a moment to realize that most of the pictures were portraits of the same person, some showing a child wearing 1950s-era clothing, others depicting a middle-aged woman in tie-dye, another representing someone who looked to be about sixty years of age, dressed in a blue gown and holding an award. Interspersed between these portraits were occasional pictures of Max, Michael, and even Isabel herself, though their faces appeared somewhat older and their clothing and hairstyles seemed utterly wrong.

Many of the portraits showed a blond girl about her own age, and Isabel instantly recognized the likeness. *Tess,* she thought before she remembered where she was. *No. Not Tess. I'm inside the mind of Jolene Skarrstin.*

One end of the corridor appeared more brightly lit than the other, and Isabel took this as a cue to move forward, approaching the light. She passed what seemed like hundreds of identical, featureless wooden doors and as many images of Skarrstin/Tess before nearing what appeared to be the corridor's end. She came to a stop at the final door.

This portal was unlike any of the others, draped with heavy chains, which were fastened with several formidable-looking iron padlocks. A bright, unearthly light spilled from beneath the door, forming a pool of cool golden radiance at her feet.

Skarrstin obviously doesn't want anyone poking around in here.

Taking a deep breath, Isabel carefully placed both hands on the cluster of chains and locks that barred her way. She concentrated, willing unfathomable energies up from the core of her being. The chains quickly grew warm against her skin, then appeared to melt into the air like so much smoke. Isabel pushed gently against the door, which slowly opened before her, allowing more of the brilliance within to flood into the corridor. Putting aside her growing feeling of trepidation, Isabel stepped inside, raising her hands to shield her eyes from the glare.

As her eyes adjusted to the light, a weird tableau began

to unfold before her. She was standing in the center of a wide, vaulted chamber whose walls were constructed of a gleaming metallic material that obviously had come from no place on Earth. A short distance away was a squat table, where Michael Guerin lay in restraints as a pair of short, gray-skinned, black-eyed alien creatures poked and prodded him with various arcane metal instruments. The creatures gave off a peculiar sour/sweet odor that Isabel found not entirely unpleasant.

Suddenly straining against the straps that held him, Michael screamed in pain and fury, a sound that chilled her to the bone.

No. It isn't Michael, she realized with a start. The agonized man before her appeared to be at least ten years older than Michael, and his clothing and hairstyle were each a good half-century out of date. She recalled the photograph of Charles Dupree she had seen at Michael's apartment. *Michael's genetic template.*

Isabel turned and saw a few more aliens enter the chamber through portals set into the gleaming walls. A little girl in a flouncy yellow dress was with the creatures, and they gently coaxed her toward a second table. Isabel recognized the girl immediately from several of the hallway portraits, as well as from snatches of her own earliest memories of Tess.

Young Jolene Skarrstin. She can't be much older than four. Any residual doubt Isabel might have harbored that Skarrstin had served as Tess's genetic template evaporated at that moment.

Little Jolene laughed as the alien creatures shepherded her onto the table. The girl was giggling, as though the aliens were merely playing some sort of game with her. Then she looked toward the table upon which Dupree lay, and her laughter abruptly ceased.

Dupree cried out semicoherently to the girl, obviously struggling to warn her to flee. But it was far too late for that. The aliens grabbed the girl, ignoring her screams and flailing limbs as they strapped her down to the table. Isabel's stomach roiled as she witnessed the little girl's escalating terror. She turned away, unable to watch any more.

Then Isabel saw several things that she hadn't noticed earlier. In a far corner of the chamber, mounted on the wall at about eye level, were a quartet of ovoid, organic-looking containers. She recognized them immediately as duplicates of the birthing pods from which she, Max, and Michael—and later Tess—had emerged more than a decade earlier, in that remote cavern in the New Mexico desert. And nearby was a sight that was even harder to explain.

It was a third table, on which lay two people, a young man and a young woman, both apparently unconscious. Though their faces were obscured by the forest of alien equipment that surrounded them, Isabel saw that the man wore a rumpled black tuxedo, while the woman was dressed in a tattered wedding dress. As she watched, their wide table swiveled and automatic mechanisms disengaged the elaborate network of restraining straps and metal probes that had kept them pinned to the table.

A bright light from overhead seized the wedding couple with a tangible solidity, like a giant hand plucking a grape from a vine. Within the shaft of light, small globules of blue, gelatinous material began spinning about the bodies of the captives, spattering on their skin and clothing. The newlyweds floated in the air before Isabel's horrified eyes, apparently waking up as spasms of intense pain wracked their bodies and contorted their faces.

Then Isabel noticed something on the floor near her feet. A wallet and a purse, discarded, their contents scattered about the floor. She knelt and found a driver's license that bore the likeness of a very familiar face, as well as a name she had heard before: DARRYL MORTON.

Isabel stepped forward to get a better look at the pain-distorted faces of the two people floating in the beam. There was no mistake.

That's Max's face. And mine. She studied the two floating figures and considered the tuxedo and the wedding gown. Revulsion surged within her.

No. It can't be. They were married. Or about to get married.

Isabel wondered if she was witnessing the procedure the aliens had used to hybridize their unearthly genetic material with that of their human captives. Would Charles Dupree and little Jolene soon endure the same thing? She hated to think that her own origin might have inflicted such agony on anyone. Tears flooded her eyes.

Having seen more than enough, Isabel turned toward the door, moving quickly back in the direction from which she had come. She noted with some relief that the portal hadn't vanished. It was still open, just as she had left it.

But before she reached the threshold, the light of a tremendous explosion suffused the room. In eerie silence, a great gray-and-orange mushroom cloud appeared in the outer corridor, rising to the heavens like an unstoppable force of nature. A moment later the shockwave struck her, knocking her backward. It seized her by the shoulders, shook her, and threw her like a rag doll, until—

"Isabel!"

She came back to the real world with a start, realizing that someone was holding her shoulders and shaking her. "Isabel!" It was Max's voice, sounding as scared as she'd ever heard him. How long had he been calling her name, trying to rouse her?

"I'm . . . I'm okay, Max," she said, gasping for air. She realized she was shivering—and most definitely *not* okay—and that she was still in the Chevy, though she was smashed up against the door, as if recoiling from something horrible. She noticed that Kyle was still sitting in the back of the car, leaning forward and watching her anxiously. Looking down, she saw the fishing photo of Jolene Skarrstin that still lay in her lap.

Bits and pieces of her dreamwalk came flooding back to her. "Jolene Skarrstin is definitely Tess's DNA donor," she said, catching her breath. "There's no doubt about that. I saw her memories of her abduction. My God, she was only a little girl. . . ."

Isabel forced herself to rein in her emotions, to keep the horror of what she'd seen from overwhelming her.

"What else did you see?" Max asked.

Her breathing growing steadily more normal, Isabel said, "I saw our genetic templates there as well, Max. Yours and mine. Charles Dupree, too. I think their DNA was being extracted, to create the four of us. And . . . the aliens were exposing their captives to the Gandarium."

"Gandarium," Max said, frowning thoughtfully. "The aliens must have been using the Gandarium to bridge the gap between our genes and those of their captives. Just like Brody's 'friend' Larek explained."

"I don't get it," Kyle said. "You guys told me that Larek said that the Gandarium can infect only about one in—what was it?—fifty million humans. Without a particular genetic flaw, our Earthling genes don't mix very well with your cosmic RNA, Gandarium or no. Seems like the aliens would have had a tough time finding exactly the right people to snatch without attracting a lot of unwanted attention."

Max shrugged. "Maybe the Gandarium can only operate on people with the gene flaw when it's operating on its own to try to take over the world. Maybe it works differently when a bunch of alien scientists are using it as a lab tool. Or maybe they even used it on our templates to *give* them the genetic flaw that Charles Dupree had."

"So Skarrstin and whoever donated the DNA to make you and Isabel all probably had the same flaw," Kyle said, "created deliberately by the aliens."

"Liz can probably help us sort that one out later," Max said.

Suddenly recalling another detail from her dreamwalk, Isabel cut in. "I saw the name of your genetic template, Max." She struggled for a moment to retrieve those names; as with actual dreams, the details of dreamwalks sometimes tended to fade away afterward.

"Morton," she said finally. "Darryl Morton. And there was a woman with him who looked like me."

"Christine Morton," Max said, his eyes wide.

Isabel thought she recognized the name. "Weren't their

names on that list you and Liz put together?"

Nodding, Max pulled out his cell phone and flipped it open. "I've got to tell Liz about this. Those names were in Dupree's diary, along with Skarrstin."

"Do you think Dr. Skarrstin knows where to find those people today?" Kyle asked. "If they're still alive, I mean."

Isabel nodded, recalling the portrait gallery she had seen at the start of her dreamwalk. Some of those pictures had to have been of the Mortons. "I'm almost sure of it."

Kyle gave her a wry grin. "Well, then. You two certainly seem to be on the right track for a family reunion. Judging from her reaction, she obviously remembers the Mortons."

"And she seemed pretty terrified about that when she saw us in her office," Max said. To Isabel, he said, "Can you remember anything else important?"

Isabel recalled the way the Mortons had been dressed. They were obviously newlyweds, or a couple on their way to elope. Her stomach heaved with a creepy feeling. Though she hated concealing anything from Max, she shook her head.

"There were a few weird images," she said. "But I think those were mostly weird subconscious things, or maybe dream symbols."

"I'm pretty good with dream interpretation," Kyle said, an eager look on his face.

Putting aside the implications of the Mortons' wedding attire, Isabel wrestled with yet another troubling dreamwalk image.

"All right, Dr. Freud," she said to Kyle as Max began dialing Liz's number. "What do you suppose a gigantic nuclear bomb blast symbolizes?"

15

The night had been uncomfortable for Michael, Maria, and Liz. After they returned to Maria's house from the Crashdown, Amy DeLuca had allowed Michael to stay over, as long as he slept on the couch. Liz stayed over as well, sleeping in Maria's bed, just like they had done growing up when sleepovers had been filled with more fun and innocence.

Several times during the night, Maria heard Amy getting up for water or to go to the bathroom, or because of some other excuse, but even half asleep, Maria knew why her mother had really risen. *She wants to make sure Michael and I are behaving ourselves.* Little did she know that they had already been intimate, the first time on the evening before the Pod Squad was supposed to leave Earth in the Granilith.

Early in the morning, Maria awoke to an odd sight. Michael was squatting beside her bed, looking at her with a goofy grin on his face. "What's so funny?" she asked, one hand subconsciously wiping the side of her mouth where she knew she had probably drooled on her pillow.

"Nothing's funny," Michael said. "I was just enjoying watching you sleep."

"Sure, you were just hoping for some girl-on-girl action, weren't you?"

He mimed being shot in the heart. "You wound me, milady."

Yawning, she noticed the morning sunlight coming in through the bedroom drapes. "What time is it?"

"Haven't looked yet. It's still early. I couldn't sleep very well. I'm kind of restless. Well, *really* restless."

Maria knew that they were supposed to meet Valenti sometime this morning for coffee, to discuss the afternoon's pending events. Thinking of her mother's concern last night about who was sleeping with whom, she found herself idly wondering where Amy's sometime boyfriend had spent the night.

"Where and when are we supposed to meet with Valenti again?" Maria asked. She felt fuzzy, sleep still enfolding her brain like a blanket.

"At the Crashdown at nine-thirty." Michael hesitated a moment, then added, "Can you get up and drive me someplace first?"

"Hmmmm, let me consider the options," Maria said. "More sleep, or drive my potentially psychopathic boyfriend somewhere on the day of his big trial?"

An angry shadow passed over Michael's face. "It's not a trial, Maria. It's only a hearing. The trial comes later, after the Hanging Judge throws me back behind bars."

Maria immediately regretted her big-mouthed wit. "Michael, I'm sorry, it was a joke."

He stood up, brushing her hand away from his arm. "No, don't worry about it. I can deal with things on my own." He stalked out of the room.

Maria beat her head on the pillow, then shook Liz awake. "Liz, wake up. We gotta take Michael someplace."

"Huh?" Liz was still very much out of it.

Maria pulled on some sweatpants and a comfy pair of slip-on shoes. "Come on! We gotta get up!" She grabbed Liz's shoes and tossed them onto her supine form. Liz yelped and began to come more fully awake.

Maria left the bedroom, just in time to see Michael go out the front door. She ran back to the bedroom. "Hurry up, Liz!" Liz sleepily pulled her shoes on and reached for her jacket.

Moments later, the two girls were out of the house, but Michael was already nearly a block away, walking quickly. Liz got in the backseat of the Jetta, and Maria pulled out of the driveway. They pulled up next to Michael as he stalked down the street, a gloomy expression on his face.

Maria rolled down the window and called to him, "Michael, come on. Get in the car." He turned and glared at her, then continued walking as before. Maria pulled the car forward. Michael stepped off the curb and prepared to cross the street, but Maria pulled forward again, turning the wheel and stopping inches from Michael's foot.

"You're crazy, Maria," Michael said, glowering down into the car. "You could have run over my foot."

"Waaaaah," Maria retorted, mimicking the sound of a crying infant. It wasn't one of her trademark snappy come-backs, but she was too tired to try any harder. "Now get in the car."

Once the still-sullen Michael had clambered in beside Maria, she asked him where it was he had wanted to go. "Pohlman Ranch," he said without hesitation. "To *our* spot."

Maria flicked her eyes up to the rearview mirror. She saw that Liz had tensed up, her arms wrapped around herself.

"You mean Maideckizne Rocks, where the Granilith was?" Maria asked.

"Sort of. The overlook nearby. Where you and I went *afterward*."

As she drove, Maria glanced at him. A lump rose in her throat. "That's so sweet," she managed to choke out, trying to concentrate on keeping the car on the road despite the rush of memories.

She recalled that when the "Royal Four" had been planning to leave Earth in the Granilith a few months back, Michael had decided to stay behind at the last minute. Exiting the Granilith, he had run into Liz, Maria, and Kyle, who had informed him that Tess had killed Alex. Later, after Tess had taken off in the Granilith, Michael and Maria had walked together to a ridge overlooking the night-draped desert. There they had held each other tightly, until dawn painted the land in the sharp colors of blood and earth.

Through her tears, Maria looked over and saw that Michael seemed uncomfortable witnessing her display of emotion. She slid her hand over and clasped his hand.

In silence, they continued driving down the lonely desert road.

* * *

Liz was extremely uncomfortable being at Pohlman Ranch. What this area represented was painful. It was here that Max had come with Tess and Isabel and Michael, planning to leave her—and the world they had always known—behind. The last time she had come here she had told the aliens that Tess was a killer. Despite that revelation, Max had let Tess go. Tess had taken his unborn child within her and left Earth, and Liz knew he mourned the loss keenly even now.

No, it's his son *that he mourns losing, not Tess.* It was small comfort, but the thought still provided some relief for her bruised heart and soul. Max had tried to repair their relationship during the time since, but it was so hard to figure out what she wanted . . . and what she could permit herself to *have.*

The Max from the future had told her that if she stayed with Max, Earth would be taken over by aliens, and that all would be lost. Future Max had claimed that Tess was critical to the survival of the race, because the "Royal Four" could not exist as a complete unit without her. "We all had different gifts," Future Max had said, "and with one of us missing, we weren't as strong, and everything fell apart."

And now, Tess *was* gone anyhow, and the unit was no more. So even though she had faked sleeping with Kyle in order to hurt Max so badly that he would fall out of love with her, had Liz's sacrifice been for nothing? If Tess had been destined to leave no matter what, why was it necessary for Max and Liz to break up? Was destiny immutable?

She was suddenly pulled back into the present by a crack of thunder. Even in the newly arrived daylight, she couldn't see any flames or plumes of smoke against the blue morning sky. Another explosion followed, and then a third. Keeping low, Liz ran toward the sound, painfully aware that it was coming from the direction of the overlook. The spot to which Michael and Maria had gone.

Peering around a rock outcropping, Liz jumped again when the sound from a fourth explosion split the air. And now she saw what it was, as a shower of dust and rock fragments began settling to the ground. Maria sat on the edge of the overlook, her fingers plugging her ears. Michael stood in front of her, his arms raised, his hands faintly glowing with power. He pointed a hand at another small boulder, which fissured open with a loud report before exploding into rubble.

"Hey!" Liz yelled, stepping out into the open. Michael turned to look at her, and seeing his actions, Maria did as well. "Not exactly low profile, Michael!" Liz said. She stalked closer to them, until they could hear her normal voice. "We don't know who else is out here. What if Hanson's people have been watching us? Do you really want some sheriff's deputy to see you blowing up rocks out here?"

"I was just . . . I needed to get this energy out of my system," Michael said, lowering his no-longer-glowing hands. "All day yesterday and all night it's been building up inside me. Better here than in front of Judge Lewis."

He began to walk forward, toward one of the crumbled targets of his powers. "I've got so much inside me that can hurt. Even back on Antar I was a military general. My whole reason for *being* seems to be to enact violence. But I could *never* use it against him. I never *did* use it against him. No matter *what* he did to—" His voice broke off, and he fell to his knees.

Maria was on her feet and running toward him as quickly as she could, and Liz moved closer as well. Michael's shoulders trembled, and Liz could hear his ragged breath, and his quiet sobbing.

Maria knelt in front of him and pulled him into her arms, cradling his head against her chest. She rubbed him on the back as he wept.

Liz felt awkward for a moment, but then knew—with a clarity that surprised her—that Michael needed to feel loved and befriended now more than ever. She knelt in the desert sand next to him and Maria, and put her arms around him from behind. He began to cry harder then, his sobs moving out into the dry desert air. Liz leaned her head on his back, feeling Maria's hands under her cheek.

After several minutes, Michael got quieter and calmer. He began to sit up, and Maria and Liz let go of him. He wiped at his eyes with the backs of his hands. "I'm sorry," he said. "I'm being a total wimp."

"Hey," Maria said sharply, and took his hand. "I love my wimp." She paused for a second for dramatic effect, and added, "*Most* of the time. Besides, Spaceboy, those tears only prove that you're way more human than you give yourself credit for."

He smiled weakly. "All those years I put up with him. My foster mother married him. Then when she went to prison, he just kept me on for the monthly checks from the county."

Liz had never heard Michael speak about his family much, but given that his last name was different from

Hank's, she assumed that someone else must have taken him in before Whitmore had.

"I learned really quickly how to stay out of his way," Michael said. "Especially when he was drunk. Which was most of the time. The first time my powers showed up was when he took a belt to me for breaking one of the dishes when I was washing them. He was hitting me and hitting me, and then the whole rack of drying dishes exploded. He got a scar above his left eye from the fragments. He left me alone for a while after that. I didn't know I had caused the dishes to explode until later."

Michael drew his legs in front of himself and crossed them. "So, then I come to find out that I'm an alien military guy on that other world. Guess I'm good with weapons and fighting and figuring out ways to do damage. Stands to reason that's how I'd develop here on Earth, too. Hank loses control, Michael loses control. Hank's a no-good drunk, Michael's a no-good—"

Maria smacked him on the hand sharply, then enfolded both his hands between her own. "*Hey!* You can talk about how crappy your d—how crappy *Hank*—was to you all you want. But kindly leave *yourself* out of that picture, okay?"

Michael looked her squarely in the eyes. He seemed almost preternaturally calm. "Maria, can you tell me, truthfully, that you didn't wonder for a moment whether I was the one who killed Hank?" He turned to look at Liz, and she could see in his eyes the sadness he so often buried beneath a veneer of tough-guy aggressiveness. "Can *you*, Liz?"

Grasping for the right words, she fidgeted for a

moment before she responded. "Michael, *anyone* would wonder, at least for a second or two. But that doesn't mean I think you killed him."

He withdrew his hands from Maria's and held them both up in front of him. "Why *not*? Every time I get angry, I lose control. And when I lose control *too* much, I blow things up. That's my power. I don't heal people, Max does. I don't dreamwalk them, like Isabel. I don't play Jedi mindwarp tricks on them, the way Tess did. No. I *destroy* things!"

"Didn't Nasedo say you would all develop more powers as you went along?" Maria asked.

"Yeah. And he also said that we were programmed to be several thousand years ahead of humankind, and able to use our full brain capacity. I guess *my* programming didn't take. I probably won't even graduate next year 'cause I'm too stupid, and every time I'm angry I go out of control and either start fights with Max or Isabel or you or my teachers. And if I'm feeling really trapped, I make things explode!"

"Michael, things have been really difficult for all of us over the last two years," Liz said. "We've all seen and done some pretty awful things."

"But in the end, *you* can go back to your life and things will be okay for you eventually," Michael said.

He turned to Maria, and Liz saw her almost imperceptibly flinch from him. "You, too, Maria. You're *normal*. I'm not. I'm a half-human, half-alien freak, and if my genetic coding hasn't *already* made me violent enough, I had it beaten into me all my life how much of a screw-up I was."

Maria covered her face with her hands and inhaled

deeply several times. Liz knew it was her relaxation technique. Finally, she removed her hands, and Liz saw tears—as well as a fire every bit as intense as Michael's explosive powers—in her eyes.

"Listen to me, Michael. Do you think I'm *stupid*?"

"No, I—"

She cut him off. "That was both a real question and a rhetorical one. I am *not* stupid. And neither is Liz. And neither was Alex. And neither is Valenti. Or Kyle. Or Liz's dad. Or my mom. Every single one of those people *believes* in you. Believes that you are *worth* their time and their energy and—in some cases—their *love*.

"Your dad screwed you up," Maria continued. "So show that you can beat him. Show the world that you're a better man than they think. Because you *are* better than most people might think. And you aren't some DNA-enslaved replicant who is fulfilling some preprogrammed mission instead of charting his own personal destiny. You don't need to be the product of your environment *or* your genes. *Screw* your stepdad. *Screw* your armies on Antar."

Still on her knees, she scooted closer to him. Cupping his chin in her hand, she forced him to look into her eyes. "Be *Michael*. Be the guy I fell in love with. Who I'm *still* in love with no matter how many times this relationship feels like a trampoline inside a tornado. *Be. Michael.*"

Liz realized that she had been holding her breath ever since Maria had started to speak. She abruptly let it all out in a great rush. Neither Michael or Maria noticed. Their eyes were still interlocked.

Liz stood, moving away to give them some privacy, and was startled when her cell phone started to ring. She answered it quickly, her voice hushed as she continued walking away from Michael and Maria. "Hello?"

"Hi, Liz. It's me." The tiny speaker made Max's voice sound small and grainy.

Liz found that seeing Michael and Maria reaching out to each other had put her in a forgiving mood; the pique she had felt earlier toward Max because of his sudden departure without her had mostly evaporated. "Hi yourself, Max. How did you sleep?"

"All right, I guess. The three of us spent the night in a little motel just outside Santa Fe. Kyle has been putting Isabel through some sort of Buddhist catechism all morning. And I think the desk clerk wants me to move in with him."

"What?" Liz asked, startled.

"Nothing. Is Michael prepared for the hearing?"

"As prepared as he'll ever be, thanks to Valenti's visit last night and a pep talk from Maria this morning. And Valenti is going to meet with us once more before showtime."

"Good. Tell Michael I believe in him." Max seemed impossibly far away, as though he were speaking to her all the way from Antar. She tried to banish the thought, without much success.

"I will. So how goes the snipe-hunt?" she said, eager to hear his voice again.

"It's been a mixed bag so far. Isabel used a photograph to dreamwalk Dr. Skarrstin and found out she's had some contact with Darryl and Christine Morton. And we've even managed to locate Skarrstin herself."

"And what does she have to say?"

"We don't know yet. She ran away and disappeared the moment she saw us. Makes me think she might be up to no good. Just like Tess."

Liz hated hearing him utter Tess's name. Then she thought about the things Maria had said to Michael about choosing one's own destiny. Those thoughts guided what she said next. "Max, you really don't have a very good idea of what Dr. Skarrstin is like—other than the fact that she seems to spook easily."

"Maybe she has something to hide."

"Maybe. Or maybe she's afraid of something."

"What are you saying, Liz?"

"Just that you probably shouldn't let your bad feelings toward Tess make you assume that Skarrstin is evil, too. Just because they share some of the same genes doesn't make them the same person."

Liz looked off into the distance, where Michael and Maria seemed to be sharing a placid, gentle moment, staring off together into the blue dome of the sky. "Nature doesn't always trump nurture, Max," she said.

Silence crackled on the other end of the line, until Liz wondered if she'd lost the connection.

"Max?"

"I'm still here, Liz. I was just thinking about what you said. Maybe you're right. Maybe I'm looking at Skarrstin through Tess-colored glasses. Anyway, I guess we'll get to the truth of it pretty soon. We're heading over to her house now. Maybe she'll agree to talk to us this time."

She heard the edge of obsession that underlay Max's tone. It was something that became noticeable whenever he thought carefully about the persistent mysteries of his alien heritage. And it was more noticeable since he had lost his unborn son. Where Michael used to be the one obsessed with their alien natures, Max was increasingly overtaking him in that role. "Good luck, Max," she said quietly.

"Thanks."

"And be careful." She wanted to say more, but didn't want to risk driving him even further away.

His laugh was gentle quicksilver. "Liz, Dr. Skarrstin might be part Tess, but I really don't think she's *dangerous*. She's, like, I dunno, *sixty* or something. What could happen?"

They said their farewells and rang off. A great pit of apprehension yawned wide inside her as she slowly walked back toward Michael and Maria.

What could happen?

16

Standing in the foyer just outside Dr. Skarrstin's front door, Max wondered why the scientist shouldn't be even more frightened to see them here than she had been back at the university. Still, there was no alternative to trying again to speak to her. He watched anxiously as Isabel punched the doorbell button, and rolled his eyes when he heard the chime. The echoing bell tones mimicked the five-note alien theme from *Close Encounters of the Third Kind*.

"Sounds like she's been expecting a visit from you wild and crazy Czechoslovakians for a long time now," Kyle whispered, grinning lopsidedly at Max. "Maybe she wants you two to feel right at home."

"Or maybe she's just a sci-fi fan," Isabel said.

I wouldn't have expected that, Max thought. *Tess was never much into that stuff. Of course, she lived it, didn't she?*

After getting no response to a second ringing of the doorbell for nearly a minute, Max rapped firmly on the door.

"I don't think anybody's home," said Isabel.

Max nodded in agreement, then placed a hand on the doorknob. Closing his eyes in concentration, he gathered his internal energies, then abruptly released them, channeling them into the lock mechanism.

The door swung silently open. Max called out Jolene Skarrstin's name and waited, but no one came to the door. And there were no sounds of movement coming from within the house.

Max favored Kyle with a lopsided grin, then started to cross the threshold. But he paused when Kyle spoke, his tone serious.

"So far, Max, it's only breaking. But if you go in there, it's breaking *and* entering."

Max tilted his head to the side, surprised at his friend's reticence. "Remember when the power went out and a bunch of us were trapped inside the UFO Center with Brody and a disembodied alien?"

"Of course. That was only a few months ago."

"Your dad told me about how you helped us that night by getting the blueprints to Brody's place out of the library."

The ex-sheriff's son shrugged. "So?"

"So how did you get into the library in the middle of the night?"

Kyle raised his eyebrows, but appeared to concede Max's point. With an ironic bow toward Skarrstin's open doorway, he said, "Go on in, then. I'll stay out in the front down here and stand watch in case Dr. Skarrstin comes back."

"Good plan," Max said. He walked inside, followed by Isabel.

Kyle cautioned him one final time. "Max, if we get caught doing this, we don't have a friend on the force here. This is Santa Fe, not Roswell."

"Then we'll just have to make sure we don't get caught," Max said just before he and Isabel ventured inside.

The main level of the compact town house looked pretty much as Max expected—the somewhat cluttered, book-filled home of an academic. Tall, wooden book-shelves lined the walls, crammed with books of every description, ranging from nonfiction volumes on archaeology, religion, medicine, and cosmology to classic science fiction novels. The mantel shelf held a few dusty knick-knacks and small sculptures from foreign lands whose cultures he didn't recognize.

"Dr. Skarrstin sure seems to read a lot more than Tess ever did," Max said, impressed. *Who'd have thought Tess had it in her?*

Isabel surveyed the combined living room–dining room area with a critical eye, running a finger along one of the book-filled shelves. "She dusts a lot less than Tess did too. Go figure."

Making their way up the stairs, Max and Isabel entered a room that seemed to be part bedroom and part office. Even more books and papers were crammed into this smaller space, with everything arranged in concentric stacks around a beat-up oak desk, atop which sat a somewhat outdated computer. *She probably can't afford to buy the newest model every year on a professor's salary,* Max thought.

Isabel suddenly tensed. "What was that?"

"I didn't hear anything."

"I thought I heard something move downstairs."

"Kyle's down there, remember? I think he'd have shouted a warning if anybody came by."

She nodded her head, looking embarrassed. "Just jittery, I guess. I don't think I'll ever get good at burglary."

He smiled. "Glad to hear it." Always having to bail Michael out of trouble was difficult enough. He didn't need his sister to become a problem child as well.

Max and Isabel began inspecting the contents of the bookcases surrounding the desk, as well as the heaps of books and papers that lay all about the workspace.

"Bingo," Max said after a few minutes. He lifted a heavy tome up so that Isabel could inspect it. On the dust jacket was a lurid, grainy photograph of a classic, disk-shaped UFO, hovering over the iconic image of a big-headed gray alien. The alien looked about as real as the inflatable souvenir alien dolls Amy DeLuca sold at the Crashdown Café.

"We must be in the right place," Isabel said, picking up a volume that showed a picture of a DNA molecule on the cover.

"Liz would go crazy in here," Max said, feeling an exhilarating rush of discovery. "It looks like Skarrstin has a whole library here on molecular biology, recombinant DNA, radiation, oncology, blood disorders . . ."

"Max, what's this?" Isabel said, kneeling to touch the books that lined a shelf near the floor.

Max knelt beside Isabel and touched the line of incongruously tidy book spines. He tried to remove one of the generic-looking red hardcover volumes from the low shelf, and was surprised to find that every spine on the shelf was fused, as though all of the books there had been glued together.

"These books are fakes," Max observed.

Isabel's brows knit together. "That doesn't make any sense. Why would a college professor have fake books in her home office?"

"Because," Max said, pushing hard on the row of false spines, "burglars usually don't bother with people's libraries. The money's better in stolen stereos and TVs."

The row of false books suddenly turned on a pivot, disappearing beneath the shelf above like a garage door folding itself open. Max and Isabel peered into the shadows that filled the now-empty lower shelf.

Max wasn't terribly surprised to see a faint gleam of metal at the back of the shelf.

"A safe," he said. He lay down on the floor to give himself better access to the safe door. Concentrating his power through his right hand, he opened the door and gently pulled a black plastic container about the size of a large school backpack from the locker's dark interior.

"She went to a lot of trouble to keep anyone from finding that," Isabel said as Max moved the box to a clear spot on the floor, sitting beside it. She knelt nearby, watching as he carefully removed the box's lid.

Inside the box lay several sealed test tubes containing a substance that appeared to be blood, though in the shadows Max could see that the fluid was suffused with a faint blue glow. Carefully removing the vials, Max found a thick stack of manila file folders, which he lifted from the box as well.

The box was now empty except for another sealed, glowing vial, this one larger than the smaller bottles of blood. He lifted it up to examine it more closely. Half oozing, half crystalline, and as blue as the desert sky, there could be no mistaking what this stuff was.

"Gandarium," they both said together.

After a moment, Isabel made a face. "That bottle looks airtight," she said. "Isn't this stuff supposed to die when it can't get any air?"

Max recalled that the Gandarium that had possessed Grant Sorenson—and had nearly suffocated Kyle Valenti and Alex Whitman during its bid to take over the world—had been killed by oxygen deprivation. He made a face that matched Isabel's. "You're right."

"So why does it look like it's still alive?" Isabel said.

"My guess is that Skarrstin has discovered something that can be mixed in with the Gandarium to keep it alive, but only just barely," Max said. "The seal on the vial must keep the stuff from getting the air and water it needs to grow out of control. Liz can probably figure it all out once we get it home."

Isabel looked appalled. "Gandarium is pretty dangerous stuff, Max. What if it accidentally gets out? Larek described it as a kind of alien virus. Do you want to be responsible for contaminating the entire planet?"

"I'll be careful with it. But do you really think we ought to trust a woman who is basically *Tess* to hold on to this stuff?"

Isabel appeared to ponder that for a moment, then nodded grudgingly. "All right. It looks like we don't have a lot of good alternatives here."

"You just said a mouthful," said a sharp voice from behind them. Startled, Max turned toward the sound.

He froze. Dr. Jolene Skarrstin stood in the doorway,

holding a large pistol in front of her with both hands. It was pointed directly at Max's head.

Skarrstin's eyes locked with Max's. "Put that vial down," she ordered, cocking the gun. "Nice and gently. Then back away from the box."

Max had no choice but to comply. "Take it easy," he said as he stepped carefully backward, empty-handed. "We haven't come to hurt you."

"Sure. First you surprise me in my office, wearing faces I haven't seen for fifty years. Then you break into my house and try to rob my safe. Should I take you in as houseguests? Bake you a cake, maybe? Adopt you?"

"What happened to Kyle?" Isabel asked. Only then did Max remember that Kyle was supposed to be standing guard out in the foyer.

"Your little friend out by the front door?" Skarrstin asked. "Big, strong, attractive kid. But he's something of a pacifist, isn't he? He ought to have a hell of a lump on his head when he finally wakes up."

Ouch. I'm never going to hear the end of this, Max thought. *Assuming we all get out of here without getting our heads blown off.*

Skarrstin's hands were shaking, and Max noticed a sheen of sweat forming on her brow. It was obvious that she was terrified. Max knew he had to calm her down fast, or else the situation could get very ugly very quickly.

"Who are you working for?" Skarrstin demanded, shaking the gun to emphasize each syllable of her query.

"We're here on our own," Max said, carefully keeping his hands out where she could see them. "We're not working for anyone. We only want to talk to you."

"About what?"

"About your past." He exchanged a quick nervous glance with Isabel, then decided to press on. "About the day the aliens took you."

The gun wavered slightly in Skarrstin's hands, though Max was uncomfortably aware that the barrel was still pointed squarely at him. Max kept both his hands up, palms pointed outward. He could see that she was frightened enough to shoot without necessarily meaning to.

Got to get a power-shield up. He felt the energy quickly building up within him.

"How do you know about the aliens?" Skarrstin said, her voice quavering.

"Please put the gun down," Isabel said. "We're not here to hurt you. We came to ask you for your help."

Skarrstin clearly had not been expecting that. She lowered the weapon an inch or two, but was still obviously hyperalert. Though this woman had to be around sixty, she was clearly no pushover. No wonder Kyle had underestimated her.

"I suppose that isn't any more unlikely than my having been picked up by aliens in the first place," the scientist said, though her eyes remained hard. *Pure Tess,* Max thought. "State your business," she said. "*Then* I'll decide whether to put the gun down."

"We've had some . . . experiences with the same aliens who abducted you," Max said. "Some of them go back to our early childhoods. Just like you."

Skarrstin took a step forward and looked them both up and down for a long moment. Then, apparently having reached some internal crossroads, she uncocked and lowered the weapon, though she continued clutching it tightly in her right hand.

"If you two weren't the spitting image of two other people those aliens grabbed, I might not be so tempted to believe you. Or I might have shot you both dead just for burgling my home."

Max reddened. "We're sorry about that, ma'am." He gestured toward the vial of Gandarium, where it lay in its box on the floor about four feet away from him and Isabel. "But all we're really interested in is information about the aliens."

"And the people they abducted," Isabel added.

Still suspicious, Skarrstin moved the box containing the vials from the floor to her desk. She had not yet put away the gun. Max could see that he still had to win her over.

He reasoned that the only way to get information was to share some of his own.

"The Gandarium is the key to what the aliens did to you and the others, isn't it?" Max said, recalling what Isabel had told him of her dreamwalk within Skarrstin's mind.

Skarrstin appeared puzzled. "Gandarium?"

"The glowing, blue crystal-jelly stuff in that beaker. That's what the aliens call it."

"You mean the biomorphic plasm," Skarrstin said, a tinge of wonder coloring her voice. "Well, it stands to reason that people from another star would have a different name for it."

"How did you get it?" Isabel wanted to know.

"Alien abductees sometimes have traces of the material in their bodies."

Max was beginning to understand. *So she got her first Gandarium specimens from people who've been used as genetic templates for human-alien hybrids. People like Charles Dupree, or the Mortons.*

Or like Skarrstin herself.

"Years ago," the scientist continued, "I isolated the material and discovered how to grow cultures of it under the right conditions."

"That's amazing," Isabel said. "The only other time we came into contact with Gandarium, it came directly from an alien ship."

"If you've been exposed to this stuff before, then you're both lucky to still be alive."

Max nodded. "We know. It reproduces very quickly when it has access to air and water. Take away its oxygen and it dies."

"Very good," Skarrstin said, evidently impressed by his knowledge. "Biomorphic plasm is both hard to keep alive and hard to keep from trying to kill everything in the biosphere once you get it reproducing."

"So why did you bring it home with you?" Isabel said. "Aren't you endangering the entire planet by keeping it here?"

Skarrstin smiled, shaking her head. "Over the years I've developed some novel methods of keeping the plasm's growth in check. What you see here is a mutated strain of the—what did you call it? Gandarium?—that can't reproduce without the assistance of a very rare synthetic amino acid."

"Like those dinosaurs in *Jurassic Park*," Isabel said wonderingly. Max winced, recalling how badly that particular precaution had failed the dinosaur-makers in the film.

"Something like that," Skarrstin said, chuckling.

"What do you recall about the day you were abducted?" Max asked. "Anything you can remember might be important in helping us sort out our own . . . experiences."

Skarrstin paused, her eyes unfocused. Though she still held the gun, she clearly wasn't thinking about anything going on in the room at the moment.

"I was only five years old," she began after she had finished gathering her thoughts. "Young enough so that I sometimes look back on the experience almost as a dream. But not quite. It really happened to us."

"You weren't the only one abducted," Isabel said. She wasn't asking a question.

"No. There were others. It all seemed like a nightmare, but after it was over, there we stood, out in the desert where the aliens released the four of us. We were naked, hungry, and in pain from their medical tests and cell-sample extractions."

Max had a fair idea of what Skarrstin had suffered, based on his experiences at the hands of the sadistic FBI Agent Daniel Pierce, who had come very close to dissecting him in the Eagle Rock military facility's secret "White Room."

"It sounds terrible," Max said, his voice scarcely above a whisper. "It must have taken a long time for you to recover."

She smiled at that, and for the first time Max saw a glint in her eyes that might have signaled the flare-up of decades-old madness. Perhaps she had *never* truly recovered from her traumatic capture as a child.

"It didn't take as long as you might think for us to heal," Skarrstin said. "Physically, at least. Within a day none of us had a mark anywhere on our bodies. There was no evidence that anything had ever happened to us, other than the memories we carried. And none of us had a sick day for decades afterward. While we all got older as the years went by, we felt healthy and vigorous for decades, more like people half our age. I suppose that's a fringe benefit of the traces of biomorphic plasm they left in our cells."

Isabel wore a thoughtful expression. Max could tell she was doing her best to keep Skarrstin talking. "The Gandar—the biomorphic plasm—might not have kept all of you as healthy as you think," Isabel said. "Our friend Laurie Dupree inherited a genetic defect from her grandfather, Charles Dupree—"

"A defect caused by the plasm," Skarrstin said.

Looks like I was right, Max thought, recalling the alien Larek's explanation that the Gandarium was essential for hybridizing human and alien DNA. *The aliens must have used the Gandarium to alter their captives' DNA before extracting it for the hybridization procedure. That's how they made the two types of DNA compatible.*

Skarrstin continued. "When I was in graduate school I recontacted Dupree and the Mortons, and they agreed to let me study them for aftereffects of the abduction experiences. I've documented Dupree's DNA flaw, along with all the other subtle genetic changes the aliens made to each of our bodies. That's how I eventually isolated the biomorphic plasm. I've studied dozens of other abductees. But we four were the only ones whose bodies contained the plasm."

"I bet the government would love to get their hands on your work," Max said, watching her reaction carefully.

Isabel sniffed with disdain. "They'd probably just try to make some sort of weapon out of it."

"They'd need what I keep up here to do that," Skarrstin said, tapping her skull with a long, delicately tapered finger. "And I've never had any interest in using what I've learned to kill people. They'd have to kill *me* first."

That sounded to Max like an invitation to ask another question. "So what *do* you use your research for?"

Skarrstin's face lit up with an almost fanatical enthusiasm. "Cancer therapies, young man. Were you aware that the old A-bomb tests during the nineteen fifties have ballooned cancer rates all across the Southwest?"

Max nodded. *That accounts for the atomic explosion Isabel saw in her last dreamwalk.*

"Small children are the most vulnerable," she continued, "especially to diseases like leukemia and multiple myeloma. But I think the plasm-altered cells of abductees like myself might hold the key to a cure. This material has kept me and the Mortons healthy all these years; think what it might do for others."

Max thought of his own innate power to repair bodily injuries and cure diseases, and how he had used that ability last Christmas to heal a hospital ward full of terminally ill children, including Brody Davis's little daughter, Sydney. *If the Gandarium is the ultimate source of that power, then maybe Skarrstin really is on the right track.*

"I've researched the abduction literature rather thoroughly as well," Skarrstin continued. "Partly to avoid being captured again by aliens. That's why I've tried to keep what they did to me a secret all these years. You see, I know there are plenty of others besides the government who might try to wipe out my research, or pervert it into some kind of weapon."

"I don't doubt it," Max said, wondering where she was going with this.

"For instance, did you know there's a race of extraterrestrials who've made their presence known by leaving their shed skins lying around?"

Max nodded, though he wasn't eager to go into detail about just how much he really knew about the ruthless alien adversaries he and his friends knew as the Skins.

"Strange," Skarrstin said slowly. "There aren't that many who know of them. Other than federal agents. Or other aliens."

She raised the gun and cocked it again in a single fluid motion. Once again, Max found himself looking down the weapon's broad barrel.

Skarrstin's eyes blazed with paranoia and renewed rage. "After all these years, you've finally found me *again*. But your mistake was taking on the forms of Darryl and Christine."

Max raised his hands. "No, I promise you. We're not—"

Before he could utter another word, Jolene Skarrstin pulled the trigger.

17

Jesse Ramirez still hadn't gotten used to the hard wooden benches in the courtrooms at the Chaves County Court-house. They felt more like church pews than seats. So he was glad when Judge Lewis had announced that the after-noon's events were to take place in his rather spacious chambers rather than in a courtroom, which would have had to be sealed due to Michael's status as a minor.

At first, Jesse had thought it was odd that they would hold an evidentiary hearing in chambers, but Phillip Evans had explained to him that Lewis did things a bit dif-ferently than most. "He's a fine adjudicator, and very fair, but sometimes he prefers to dispense with the pomp and circumstance," Phillip had told him at their breakfast meeting. "Don't be surprised if he cuts you off with some colloquialism if he thinks you're rambling."

Jesse was also surprised at how roomy Lewis's cham-bers were. The few times he had been in chambers while at Harvard, the rooms had been fairly cramped and stuffy. He was always amused at how realistic the sets for the TV show *The Practice* had been, since he had often found himself in chambers, courtrooms, and meeting rooms exactly like those portrayed on the series.

Compared with the Boston judges, Lewis was living large. He had several leather-upholstered chairs, as well as animal-head trophies mounted on the walls. Jesse recognized a reproduction of a painting by the famed cowboy artist Charles Russell on one wall, and was amused to see a set of golf clubs in the corner, half hidden behind the coatrack that held Lewis's robes. Jesse wondered if Phillip's long history with Lewis extended beyond the bar and onto the greens.

Seated next to Jesse was Michael Guerin, and the boy was flanked on the other side by Phillip. Jesse was pleased to note that Michael had cleaned up nicely; though he hadn't overdone it with a suit and tie, he did have a dress shirt and slacks on, and his hair was neatly combed back. More than that, Jesse noted that Michael was radiating a pure sense of calm.

To Jesse's left, in another trio of chairs facing the desk, were District Attorney Jenique Mabell, Sheriff Randall Hanson, and State Police investigator Daniel Lubetkin. Seated next to the Judge's desk was Betsy McDaniel, the feistiest septuagenarian court reporter Jesse had ever seen.

The others were all waiting outside: ex-Sheriff Jim Valenti, Maria DeLuca and her mother, Amy, Diane Evans, and Jeff and Elizabeth Parker. They would be called in as character witnesses if needed. At the very least, Jesse expected that Valenti would be questioned.

The side door to chambers opened and Lewis came barreling in, removing a vintage leather bomber jacket and hanging it on the coatrack, over his robe. "Sorry to keep y'all waiting. My morning constitutional needed a little *amendment* this morning."

Jesse laughed slightly, and was pleased to note that Michael had as well. A quick glance showed that Lewis saw Michael's smile, and that only the D.A. on the opposing counsel side was similarly amused. *Score one point for laughing at the judge's jokes,* Jesse thought.

"Now then," Lewis said, sitting down. "I decided to have this little session in chambers rather than in a sealed court not only because it seems a bit more comfortable, but also because I'm not sure this entire matter merits an evidentiary hearing. So, we're still going to follow protocol, and if the evidence supports the need for further proceedings, I'll schedule them."

Lewis turned to the court reporter. "Everybody sworn in who needs it, Betsy?" She nodded.

He looked pointedly over at D.A. Mabell. "Now from what I see, there isn't much evidence here, Ms. Mabell, and questions of a formal hearing may soon be moot. So why don't we start with you?"

Mabell started to stand, then apparently realized she didn't need to. "Your Honor, yesterday the remains of Henry Whitmore were discovered buried in the desert. His body had been burned by unknown means, and we are not able as yet to precisely determine the cause of death. There is, however, a large handprint scorched into his chest."

Lewis raised an eyebrow, but said nothing, so Mabell continued. "Mr. Guerin was Whitmore's foster son. We have multiple documented cases of Whitmore physically abusing the boy, as well as three wives and assorted girl-friends. On the last day anyone saw Mr. Whitmore alive, neighbors heard shouting, screaming, and gunfire in the trailer where Mr. Whitmore and Mr. Guerin lived. The next day, Whitmore did not go to his job, nor was he seen by anyone. Shortly after that, Mr. Guerin was arrested by then-Sheriff James Valenti, but he was released O.R., due to an alibi provided by a Ms. Amy DeLuca."

Mabell cleared her throat and checked her notes, tossing the judge a quick look before she resumed. "During this time, Your Honor signed an emancipation order for Mr. Guerin, even though the father had yet to be found. Later that evening, Sheriff Valenti claimed that he was visited by Mr. Whitmore, who informed him that he was going to take a new job in Las Cruces, and that he would be taking his trailer with him. Mr. Whitmore never showed up for his new job, nor did he ever take possession of the trailer. In fact, other than Sheriff Valenti, Henry was never seen by anyone until his corpse was discovered."

Lewis breathed deeply, then let it out audibly through his nose. He squinted, pondering for a moment. "Is that *it*, counsel? You have no further evidence?"

"We have not *yet* been able to find any specific physical evidence linking Mr. Guerin to Mr. Whitmore's death. However, Sheriff Hanson and his men are still combing the site, as well as the trailer."

"Seems to me that evidence would be awfully hard to find in the desert, over a year after the fact," Lewis said. "And if that trailer's been sold as abandoned, as my paper-work indicates, any evidence there has probably been cleaned up as well."

Mabell nodded solemnly. "Yes, Your Honor. We do, however, also have evidence that suggests Sheriff Valenti may be covering for the boy. Mr. Valenti is engaged in a relationship with the mother of Mr. Guerin's girlfriend, and according to Sheriff Hanson's surveillance, Valenti has spent an inordinate amount of time with the boy both *prior* to his arrest yesterday, and *since* then. Including, I'm told, a meeting this morning." She put her notes down.

"You done now?" Lewis asked. After she nodded, he swiveled his chair and turned to Jesse. "Well, Mr. Ramirez, let's hear your side."

Jesse didn't look at his notes—he had taken a memorization course while still a prelaw undergrad—and instead looked directly at Lewis. "Ms. Mabell's case is built entirely on supposition and suspicion, with no basis in fact or evidence, Your Honor. Mr. Guerin does *acknowledge* that he was the victim of his father's abuse, but there is no evidence at all that he ever fought back. In fact, the post-mortem medical tests will show that with the exception of a broken bone suffered while he was resisting arrest for battery, and a finger broken on the job, Mr. Whitmore had sustained *no* injuries prior to his death."

"Except for one great big one at the very end," Lewis said, a grim smile on his lips. "The one that French-fried him to death."

Jesse nodded, taking care not to smile back. "Yes, except for that. Additionally, there are *no* witnesses that can place Mr. Guerin at the trailer at the time of the shooting and screams reportedly heard there, even though there were neighbors present in the surrounding trailers. Mr. Guerin has a solid alibi, verified by two people, as to his whereabouts the evening that Mr. Whitmore supposedly disappeared.

"And as to Mr. Whitmore's disappearance and reappearance, opposing counsel is practically suggesting that Sheriff Valenti *lied* about Mr. Whitmore's reappearance. Absent his own evidence, Valenti cannot prove that Whitmore did indeed visit his office, but they, in turn, cannot prove that he did not."

Jesse glanced quickly over at Phillip, and could see approval in the older man's eyes. "In short, Your Honor, the prosecutor has one main piece of evidence that cannot be refuted: They have the body of Henry Whitmore. It is clear that he died, and we can even be reasonably certain that somehow he was murdered—though the precise means still appear to defy explanation. It is also abundantly clear that he was buried in the desert, presumably by a person or persons who did not wish his remains to be found. However, Mr. Whitmore was not without enemies in this town, and these ranged from ex-wives to men with whom he'd clashed in barroom brawls to a neighbor whom he threatened to kill after the man had reported him to the local cable company for illegally tapping into his cable feed."

"What isn't proven—in *any* fashion or by any *evidence*—is that my client had anything to do with his ex-foster father's death, or the disposal of his body. In fact, given the sheriff's department's continual harassment of my client on several charges—all of which have been proven baseless—this latest charge almost smacks of *vendetta,* rather than smart police work."

Lewis nodded once, then adjusted his glasses. "Thank

you, Mr. Ramirez. A bit of advice for the future: When you say 'in short,' it's best not to follow up with three more minutes of defense. Save that for the final statement." He gave a brief, almost paternal smile, but it disappeared a moment later behind a hard mask. He gestured toward the door. "Would you call in Jim Valenti please, Phillip?"

Jesse watched Phillip get up and do as the judge asked, then turned to look at Michael, hoping to gauge his reaction. Michael gave him a slight smile. He was so serene that Jesse had to wonder if someone had spiked his breakfast cereal with tranquilizers.

Valenti came in, but seeing no extra chairs available, stood in the room's center, between the opposing counsels. He nodded to Judge Lewis, his face wearing a guarded smile. Betsy spoke up from her chair and swore Valenti in.

Once the swearing-in was done, Lewis spoke. "Jim, I want to ask you some questions about this case, and your involvement in it."

"Sure thing, Your Honor."

"What is your recollection of Mr. Whitmore's final visit to you?"

Valenti clasped his hands onto his belt. "He arrived in my office the evening after Mr. Guerin was emancipated. He told me that he had heard we'd put out an APB on him, and claimed that he had been in Carlsbad at a bar, where he'd gotten drunk with a woman he'd met. He explained that the gunshots in his trailer had occurred because he'd been cleaning his gun while intoxicated. He went on to inform me that he had gotten a job offer in Las Cruces and that he would be taking his trailer and leaving town.

Finally, he offered to sign papers for Mr. Guerin's emancipation if I needed him to do so. I told him it wasn't necessary—since the boy had been legally emancipated earlier that day—and asked him to make his departure from Roswell quickly."

"Did anyone see him talking with you?" Lewis leaned forward slightly, peering over the top rim of his glasses.

"No, sir. Not to my knowledge. And I never saw him again after that. Not until Sheriff Hanson showed me the corpse yesterday, that is."

"Why didn't you follow up on whether Hank left town?" Lewis asked.

"Because I really didn't want to see him again," Valenti said. "Good riddance to bad rubbish, as they say. I knew how he treated the women in his life, I knew how he treated the police, and I knew how he treated the boy. So I had no interest in seeing him again unless I couldn't avoid it."

Lewis nodded, looked down at the papers on his desk, then back up again. "Do you know who killed Hank Whitmore? Or have any ideas as to who might have?"

Valenti grinned slightly. "No, I do not know who killed him. I know it *wasn't* Mr. Guerin. I know there were a lot of people who didn't like Hank much. But there's not a person alive who I think would have killed Hank."

"Okay, Jim, thanks for your statements," Lewis said.

"Your Honor, if I may make one more statement on Mr. Guerin's behalf?" Seeing Lewis's nod, Valenti continued. "Boys don't always have the best of relationships with their fathers. There are a lot of reasons for that. In Michael's case, it was an *extreme*. None of us may ever know exactly how much Hank beat on that boy, but I'm betting it was a lot more than any of us suspect. But I've gotten to know Michael, and as I told Sheriff Hanson and Mr. Lubetkin yesterday, I like to think I've become sort of a surrogate father figure to him."

Jesse looked over at Michael and saw him looking up at Valenti, something indefinable in his expression. Valenti continued. "What I see in that boy impresses me. He has taken the worst the world has offered him, and he still keeps himself on a steady road. Sure, he gets a temper and can be a bit belligerent when provoked, but what teenage boy isn't? But I'm glad to know Michael Guerin, and I'm glad he's become a part of my life. And I'm glad that whatever baggage came from his past, Michael is becoming a *good man*." Valenti paused for a moment, then added, "Thanks. That's all I had to say."

"Thank you, Jim," Lewis said, not betraying any emotion. "You can see yourself out."

After Valenti had exited the room, Lewis rocked back in his chair, his fingers steepled under his chin. He opened his mouth to speak, but before a sound could come out, Michael spoke instead. "Excuse me, Your Honor. May I be heard?"

Jesse looked over at Phillip, his eyebrows raised, and the elder lawyer gave a bit of a shrug.

"Judging from the look on your lawyer's face, young man, he wasn't expecting you to ask that," Lewis said with a chuckle. "That's good. I like it when things aren't quite so set in stone. And Mr. Ramirez, you'll want to work on that poker face."

As Jesse blushed, Lewis gestured to Michael. "Go ahead."

"Over a year ago, you signed my petition for emancipation in that meeting room down the hall. You asked me if I was ready to take charge of my life as an adult, and reminded me that I would be solely responsible for my financial, educational, and medical decisions."

Lewis raised an eyebrow. "My words almost *exactly*. Glad you were paying attention."

Michael continued to exude his remarkable calm. "I *was* paying attention. I have a job, I have an apartment, I don't drink or do drugs . . . in fact, the only thing I think I do wrong sometimes is believe that everything is going to go worse than everyone expects. But you told me that day that I had folks with me who had an interest and a confidence in my future. You said your own decision was reflective of that. And you challenged me to live up to that faith."

Michael pointed out toward the door through which Valenti had just departed. "I have not only lived up to that faith, I believe that I have multiplied it. Sheriff Valenti was *not* my friend when I was emancipated. But he has *become* a friend. And I have others. Sometimes it's hard for me to understand that people can believe in me, that they can trust that I'll be anything more than the sum of the skeletons in my closet. But I can be. And I *am*."

He looked down at Jesse, favoring him with a small grin. "In *short,* Your Honor, not only did I *not* kill my stepfather, I am not a person who is capable of that kind of act. And I don't believe I ever will be."

Jesse smiled. He had underestimated Michael, but he wouldn't do it again. He would, however, join all of those who were backing up Michael's attempt to move his life in a positive direction.

Judge Lewis was apparently just as impressed. "Bravo, young man. Not only well said, but I believed it as well." He looked toward the lawyers on both sides. "I had already made my decision before Mr. Guerin's impassioned plea, but I believe that it's been suitably reinforced."

Lewis stared at the district attorney. "Ms. Mabell, I don't find that sufficient evidence has been presented, nor that any burden of proof has been met. Certainly not enough to hold Mr. Guerin for trial, and nowhere near enough to even bother me with *thinking* about a trial. The sheriff's department seems to have jumped to some amazing conclusions here, based on little evidence and some sloppy character suppositions. You would do well, Sheriff Hanson, to learn from the mistakes of your predecessor regarding overzealously pursuing someone in what could one day be interpreted as a personal vendetta."

Jesse looked over, and was glad to see that Hanson was blushing this time.

"And with *that,* I think this hearing is adjourned," Lewis said, pushing back from his desk with both hands and standing up.

Michael stood and asked, "Am I free to go?"

Phillip clapped his hand on Michael's shoulder. "You sure are, Michael."

Michael approached the judge and put out his hand. "Thank you, sir."

"You're welcome, young man," Lewis said, shaking Michael's hand. "I'll be keeping an eye on you to see what kind of promise your future holds. I trust you won't disappoint me."

"I'll do my best, sir."

Moments later, they all filed out of the room to greet the worried faces of Michael's assembled friends. Jesse gave a thumbs-up sign, and everyone erupted in cheers. Michael exited the room and was immediately engulfed in a hug by Maria.

D.A. Mabell pulled Jesse aside by his sleeve. "Be aware that Sheriff Hanson doesn't plan to leave this alone. He still wants to find the killer," she said. "And if the sheriff *does* find that so much as a single strand of Mr. Guerin's long brown hair is linked to this murder, you can rest assured he'll be back here. And I'm certain that Judge Lewis's mood will be far less forgiving."

"I don't doubt it," Jesse said after appraising the other lawyer for a moment. "Just be sure to warn Hanson he'd better not pull a stunt like this again with anything less. Tell him that otherwise the city's likely to have a hefty harassment suit on its hands. Fortunately, my client isn't a vindictive man. And it may interest the sheriff to know that Michael wants the killer caught as well."

She smiled at him, almost sweetly. "Oh, you can be sure I'll be keeping a tighter leash on the sheriff for the foreseeable future. I have my prosecution batting average to consider, after all, and I don't like to lose because of sloppy law-enforcement work. Well, Mr. Ramirez, it's been nice working with—well, *against*—you." She hesitated a moment, then fished her card out of a suit pocket. "I know you're new in town. If you'd like someone to show you around, give me a call."

Jesse raised an eyebrow and smiled. "Thank you. I'm seeing someone at the moment, but who knows what the future may hold?"

"Who knows indeed?" Her smile lit the hallway.

He watched as Mabell walked down the hall. Then, with a deep inhalation of musty courthouse air, he turned back to join the celebrants, and to usher them out of the hallway before the security people started getting antsy.

As Hanson and Lubetkin exited the room, Valenti fixed them with a stare. Hanson looked particularly chagrined, but Lubetkin betrayed no emotion.

"Randy, Dan, may I speak to you guys for a few minutes?" Valenti gestured toward a meeting room door just a few feet down the hall.

When they were all in the room, Valenti shut the door. They leaned against a wall, and he sat on the edge of the conference table. For a single reckless moment, Valenti considered vindicating himself by blurting out the simple truth about Max. Isabel, and Michael. But he could see from their hard stares that these men weren't yet ready to cross the gulf that yawned between them. With more than a little sadness, he wondered if they would ever be ready.

"I'm not going to say anything about today's proceedings, because I suspect that Judge Lewis said anything I'd say but in a shorter manner," Valenti said. "But I want to talk to the two of you, and get a few things out of the way now.

"Dan, you've known me for a couple of decades now. We were in the damned academy together. And Randy, you've been with me for a long time as well. And both of you know what my life has been like. My dad chased aliens so much that folks called him 'Sergeant Martian.' It ended his career, and affected his mind. And for a long time, I went down that same road. You both saw it. Silver handprints on corpses, strange lights in the sky, checking out every abduction report like it was the Holy Grail . . . Hell, if Fox Mulder were a real person I would have been his best damned friend!

"You two keep thinking that I'm still going around the UFO bend, and that that's what destroyed my career. Well, I'll tell you something, Dan. When I had to shoot Everett Hubble in self-defense, I saw what kind of life lay down that path of chasing aliens. My dad's in a loony bin and Hubble's dead because of their obsessions. I faced that tunnel, and turned away from it. I haven't looked back."

Valenti wiped a hand across his face, mopping away some sweat. "How much did you hear me talking about aliens after Hubble, Randy? Not a whole hell of a lot. I started to put my energies elsewhere. I started to put it into those kids. Some of them are in need of a good male role model. And I've been determined to do that for them.

"If you want to keep harassing me and following me, feel free. But leave the kids out of it. Other than what the D.A. said during this little kangaroo court you just tried to conduct, I don't know what you think they're guilty of. Or what you think *I'm* guilty of. But I've been trying to buck the history of my family, and help those kids at the same time."

He paused for a moment, then added, "It's too bad that everything I've done for you two throughout your lives doesn't win me any trust from either of you."

Hanson hung his head. "Sorry, Jim. It just seems like an awful lot of weird stuff goes on around you and those kids. But—"

Lubetkin interrupted him. "Yeah, weird stuff *does* happen. I told you before that I thought you were covering something up, and I still *do*. 'Old friend' or not, I've got a duty to the law, and I don't think you're giving me the whole story."

Valenti stepped over and stared Lubetkin straight in the eye. "That's the trouble with Roswell. You never do seem to get the whole story, no matter how much you want to hear it." He started to turn away, then turned back, holding up a finger as though making a point.

"You know what, though, Dan? *You're* talking conspiracies, cover-ups, weird stuff . . . sounds a lot to me like *you're* the one going down the same dangerous road my father traveled. Maybe *you* need to take a good, hard look at yourself—and make some decisions about what's real, and what exists only in your imagination."

Then Valenti turned on his heel and let himself out the door.

18

BOOM!

In the cramped confines of the bedroom-office, the first shot sounded like a howitzer, making Max's ears ring. He barely managed to get his power-shield up in time to stop the shell, which hung eerily in the air between himself and Isabel, suspended on the multicolored lines of electromagnetic force that emanated from his palms.

Dr. Skarrstin appeared unfazed by this manifestation of Max's alien power. *Great. Now she doesn't just suspect that we're aliens. Now she knows for sure.*

Skarrstin hesitated only for a split second before taking aim a second time. Max thought he might be able to stop another bullet or two before his concentration faltered and one finally got through. He wasn't sure how many bullets were in Skarrstin's gun, but felt pretty certain he was about to find out.

Do I feel lucky? Max concentrated on reinforcing his power-shield, watching Skarrstin very closely as she began squeezing the trigger.

Then something heavy collided very hard with the scientist, knocking the gun from her hand and sending her sprawling into a pile of books and papers, scattering them in all directions. Startled, Max dropped his shield. The first bullet he had suspended in flight fell harmlessly onto the carpet at his feet.

Nice tackle, Kyle, Max thought, watching as his friend wrestled Skarrstin back to the carpet as she tried to rise in search of her gun.

Isabel reacted quickly, retrieving the pistol before Skarrstin could reach it. Still on the floor, Kyle continued trying to restrain the scientist, who continued to fight him like a wildcat.

"Please," Kyle said through gritted teeth. "I lettered in wrestling. I don't want to hurt you."

"Let go of me!"

"Not until you calm d—"

Skarrstin surprised Kyle with an elbow to the belly, but he recovered quickly, effectively pinning her in a painful-looking wrestling hold. Still straining with surprising strength, she burst free again, only to slam her head against a bookshelf with a solid *thunk*. She slumped to the floor, limp and unconscious while a winded Kyle lay on his back, laboring to regain the breath that she'd knocked out of him.

Max and Isabel moved quickly toward Skarrstin, crouching on either side of her.

"She's still breathing," Max said to Isabel, his hand on Skarrstin's neck. "And her pulse is strong. She's only knocked out."

Isabel heaved a sigh of relief. "Thank God. We didn't come here to kill her."

Kyle propped himself up on an elbow, scowling. "I'm fine too, by the way. Thanks so much for asking. And as for the rescue, you're welcome."

Max ignored the barb. "You shouldn't have put yourself at risk that way, Kyle. Your dad wouldn't have been very happy with me if you'd gotten shot again."

Kyle winced, recalling the occasion when his father had accidentally shot him during a gunfight against FBI Agent Daniel Pierce. Kyle would have died that day, had it not been for Max's nearly miraculous healing powers. "I've been at risk ever since the day you Martians first landed in my life," Kyle said, getting back to his feet. "I've just learned to cultivate a Zen attitude about it."

"Speaking of Zen," Isabel said, "doesn't knocking old ladies unconscious go against your Buddhist principles?"

"Yup," Kyle said, nodding guiltily. "But so does watching my friends get shot."

"Touché," Isabel said, smiling playfully. "I guess decking Dr. Skarrstin sort of balances things out for you. After you let her kick your butt a few minutes ago, I mean. Sort of a yin and yang thing."

Kyle's expression could have turned milk into cheese. "Yin and yang are the balancing forces of the universe, Isabel. What you're talking about is 'don't get mad, get even.' It's not exactly the same philosophy."

"Got it." She bent at the waist and gave him a mock bow.

"All right," Max said, growing impatient with the banter, "Dr. Skarrstin is going to wake up soon. When she does, she's just going to want to shoot at us again. Unless—"

Evidently thinking along the same lines as Max, Isabel finished his sentence for him. "Unless I dreamwalk her again. Show her the truth about us."

"It's the only chance we have to win her over," Max said, watching as indecision played briefly across his sister's features. It was almost as if she was afraid to go ahead with it. He wondered what she had seen during her last dreamwalk that she hadn't told him about.

The moment passed. Isabel picked up Skarrstin's limp hand and began to concentrate.

Once again, Isabel found herself standing in the weird, metal-walled room with the vaulted ceiling. The aliens weren't present, nor were any human abductees being tormented on the tables, but the birthing pods she had seen last time were still in the corner, precisely where she'd seen them in her previous dreamwalk.

And Tess stood about a dozen yards away from Isabel, staring intently at the pods as though trying to divine their secrets.

No, not Tess, Isabel thought, noticing the young woman's old-fashioned beehive hairdo. *This is Jolene Skarrstin. This is how she looked maybe forty years ago.*

"Jolene?" Isabel called out.

The young woman who was and wasn't Tess turned toward her, apparently unaware of her presence until now.

"Oh. It's you," Skarrstin said, glowering. "So it wasn't enough for you to invade my home. Now you've come snooping inside my head. If you've got powers like that, it makes me wonder why you bothered resorting to burglary in the first place."

She knows I'm not just part of some dreamscape, Isabel thought, somewhat surprised. *Maybe her altered DNA lets her see things more clearly than normal humans can.* At least, she hoped that was the case. It would certainly make her job easier.

"You're wrong about us," Isabel said, spreading her hands before her in what she hoped was a nonthreatening gesture. "All I ask is that you give me a chance to prove it."

"You've stolen Christine Morton's face," Skarrstin said, folding her arms. "Seems to me that's the kind of trick only a hostile alien would pull. Why should I trust you?"

Isabel pointed toward the birthing pods, changing the subject in the hopes of getting around Skarrstin's guard. "You seem pretty interested in these."

"I saw them during my abduction, when I was a little girl."

Isabel nodded, beginning to understand. "But you never found out what they were for."

"That's right."

Closing her eyes to gather all of her powers of concentration, Isabel said, "Then let me show you."

Retrieving her own earliest memories, Isabel reached directly into Skarrstin's memories, connecting them.

Wordless, dreamlike images flashed and faded in a mnemonic fireworks display.

A birthing pod, seen from the inside.

A little girl coming awake, alone and afraid in a strange, dark place.

A long-haired female child, clothed only in a layer of alien goo as she emerged from the opening pod.

As though suddenly merged into a single being, Isabel and

Jolene faced the desert cavern that housed the four birthing pods that were part of Isabel's earliest recollections. A pair of young boys, as wide-eyed and confused as the girl, stood nearby. No one spoke. No one needed to.

But Isabel knew that Jolene Skarrstin now understood on some deep, visceral level exactly how she, Max, Michael, and—eventually—Tess had come into the world, as though she had experienced Isabel's hybrid human-alien origin firsthand, seeing it all through her own eyes.

Isabel gently disengaged her memories from Jolene Skarrstin's, who still stood before her in her own mnemonic alien-abduction dreamscape, looking uncannily like Tess.

"You really *are* an alien," Skarrstin said.

Isabel's heart sank. She had meant to win Skarrstin over. Had she merely driven her further away?

"Only a half-alien. Half of my DNA came from the . . . people who abducted you. The rest of it came from another human they took."

"Christine Morton, no doubt, judging from the resemblance," Skarrstin said. Isabel was relieved to hear wonder rather than fear in the woman's voice. "And that boy who was beside you . . ."

"Max," Isabel said.

"Max. He must have been created from the DNA of Christine's husband, Darryl."

Isabel nearly gasped aloud at this confirmation of the images she had seen in her earlier dreamwalk. How could she and Max—siblings all their lives in Roswell, as well as back on their homeworld—have been a *married* couple in an earlier existence?

No, she thought, struggling against waves of revulsion that threatened to capsize her. *Darryl and Christine Morton aren't us. And we aren't them. Max and I just happen to be carrying half their DNA.*

"And Charles Dupree must have been the . . . template for the other little boy you showed me," Skarrstin said.

"Yes. Michael's template. Mr. Dupree died seven years ago. Michael would have liked to have met him."

Skarrstin's voice grew thick with emotion. "And the aliens used my DNA to produce . . . a daughter."

"In a way, yes. Her name is Tess."

"A daughter," Skarrstin whispered. "I never took the time to have children. I wish I had. But it's too late now."

Isabel didn't know how to respond to the profound sadness she heard in Skarrstin's statement.

"The four of you," Skarrstin said, "have you known one another all your lives?"

"Max, Michael, and I have known one another since the beginning. Tess was raised . . ." Isabel considered telling her about Nasedo, Tess's alien guardian, but decided against beginning such a complicated tale. "Tess was raised someplace else. The three of us only met her for the first time last year."

"But you all found one another."

Isabel nodded. "Eventually." *But please don't ask me to tell you where she is now.*

"So there's always hope." Skarrstin reached toward Isabel, finally taking the hand she had offered earlier. "Take me away from these memories. I'm done looking backward."

"Gladly. One thing, though—will you promise not to shoot at us again once we're both awake?"

Skarrstin smiled, the glint of paranoia absent from her eyes. "I could never hurt my children. Or their friends."

Isabel concentrated, and the dreamwalk dispersed like a low morning fog.

Max watched anxiously as his sister sat on the floor beside the unconscious scientist. More than a minute passed in silence.

"She's coming around now," Isabel said, out of her dreamwalk so suddenly that it was as though she'd just snapped off a light. Startled, Max turned his attention back to Skarrstin and braced himself for Round Two.

The scientist's eyes fluttered open and she smiled, looking first at Isabel, and then at Max and Kyle. She rubbed the side of her head that had come into contact with the bookshelf. Max was relieved to note that she didn't seem to have suffered any permanent injury.

"This young woman has shown me quite a bit about you all," Skarrstin said to Max.

Carefully, Kyle helped Skarrstin back to her feet. "Meaning the four members of the Pod Squad," he said.

"Meaning the four of us who are aliens," Max said. Turning toward Isabel, he asked, "How did she know you were inside her mind?"

Isabel shrugged. "We know that the Gandarium changed the abductees' DNA. My guess is it made them sensitive to our powers."

"I'm also sensitive to when I'm not being told everything," Skarrstin said to Max. "Tell me about Tess. *All* of it."

Max glanced at Isabel, searching her face for guidance. It mirrored his own helpless expression.

I'm supposed to be King Zan of Antar. I shouldn't be afraid of telling Dr. Skarrstin the truth about her . . . daughter. Straightening, he trained his gaze back on Skarrstin.

"Back on our homeworld, Tess and I were married," Max began. He considered telling her that he and Tess were the king and queen of Antar, but decided that it might sound a little preposterous. He decided to stick with the essentials.

"Here on Earth, when we were reunited, we tried to rekindle our old relationship. But Tess was different here—maybe because of the influence of the . . . man who had raised her. Tess developed some pretty remarkable powers."

"Such as?" Skarrstin wanted to know.

"She could alter people's perceptions of reality. Make them think that something was happening when it wasn't. Or make you believe that nothing was happening, when in reality something important was actually happening right out in plain site."

"'These aren't the 'droids you're looking for,'" Kyle said, affecting a bad British accent. "That sort of thing."

Isabel shushed him.

Max ignored them both. He maintained eye contact with Skarrstin as he spoke. "But Tess went bad, Dr. Skarrstin. Even though she was carrying my unborn son, she left the planet. She abandoned me. She abandoned all of us. And before she left, she killed a close friend of ours."

Max doubted he could ever find it in himself to forgive Tess for destroying whatever future he might have had with his son—or for the murder of Alex Whitman.

Tears began welling up in Skarrstin's eyes. "You just

gave me a glimpse of the closest thing I'll ever have to a child of my own. And then you tell me that she was a bad seed."

Isabel looked sympathetic. "No. Tess made some bad choices. But she wasn't evil. She did what she had been trained to do by the person who had raised her."

Tess isn't evil? Max thought, feeling his facial muscles tighten involuntarily. *That's debatable.* He considered saying something aloud, but because of Skarrstin's presence he decided to let the matter drop.

"I wish we had better news to give you," Isabel said, looking at Skarrstin with sympathetic eyes. "I'm sorry."

"And I'm sorry we've had to burden you with so many questions," Max said. "But we have something else to ask you."

Skarrstin wiped away a tear. "Go ahead."

"Can you tell us how to reach the Mortons? If you consider yourself Tess's mother, then the Mortons are, in a way, parents to me and Isabel."

A thoughtful expression crossed Jolene Skarrstin's tear-streaked face. She lapsed into silence, apparently carefully considering what she wanted to say next. "No," she said finally.

"What?" Max was taken aback. "Can't you tell us *anything* about them?"

"I could. I *can*. But I think it might be a lot safer if I didn't."

"Safer for *whom*?" said Isabel, obviously as shocked as Max.

Skarrstin looked at her as though she were stupid. "For the Mortons, of course."

Max shook his head. "I don't get it. I thought you were starting to trust us."

"That's just the problem. I *am* starting to trust you. Maybe too much."

"Now I *really* don't follow you," Max said, feeling his frustration mount ever higher at Skarrstin's arbitrary decision.

"Suppose you really are marauding aliens, on Earth for some sinister reason? What if you've only tricked me into trusting you, using powers like the ones you described Tess as having?"

"You're afraid that we're after the Mortons for some reason," Isabel said. "That we might actually be planning to hurt them."

"So far you haven't given me any real proof that you're not trying to do just that. You *did* just climb into my mind, after all. That's *two* attempted burglaries, by my count."

"Interesting," Kyle said. "They taught us in debate class that you can't prove a negative."

Skarrstin scowled at Kyle. "Why exactly are you here again?"

Kyle looked flustered. Pointing toward his friends, he said, "I'm with them. And I used to live with your . . . daughter, before she and Max, um, got preg—"

Max silenced him a withering glare.

"I'll just be over here in the corner taking the bullets out of her gun, okay?" Kyle said, moving to a far corner of the little bedroom-office.

Isabel looked crushed. "Won't you tell us anything at all about the Mortons?"

"Are they even still alive after all these years?" Max asked.

Skarrstin nodded. "I think I can safely tell you that. They're alive, healthy, and still married. But they've been worried ever since nineteen forty-seven that the aliens might come back for them someday. So they changed their names and established new identities a long, long time ago."

Max reeled. *Married?* He looked toward Isabel, who appeared to be taking this information in stride. Clearly, she had already known that their genetic templates were a married couple, rather than siblings, as the two of them had been all their lives, both in Roswell and back on Antar. She just hadn't seen fit to tell him yet.

I guess we're not going to untangle that particular mystery anytime soon, he thought. *Not until we find another way to meet up with Darryl and Christine Morton.*

Max looked Skarrstin in the eye. Despite his frustration, he had to admit that he might have made the very same decision were he in her place, especially if the safety of his friends were at stake. Realizing that he couldn't fault her for her loyalty, his anger toward her began to dissipate.

And, he suddenly realized, some of his long-festering ill will toward Tess now seemed to be evaporating as well— thanks to the essential decency of Tess's genetic template.

"I'm glad you're someone who takes such good care of her friends," Max said to Skarrstin. *Maybe her loyalty proves that Isabel is right about Tess. Maybe Tess really isn't evil. At least not all the way to the core.*

"Nothing is more important than loyalty," Skarrstin

said, "to one's family and friends. I only wish I had been able to tell that to my . . . daughter."

Max and Isabel exchanged a glance that made it clear to each that it was time to leave. Kyle, watching from the corner, set the empty pistol on a chair and moved toward the door.

After Kyle and Isabel had filed out, Max paused in the doorway and looked back at Skarrstin. "Will you give the Mortons a message for us?"

Skarrstin appeared to debate the matter for a moment before nodding her assent.

"Thank you," Max said. "It's a message I'd like you to remember too. And it's simply this: The four of us never asked to be reborn with DNA stolen from abducted humans. I can't begin to tell you how much the whole idea of your abduction horrifies us. But three of us have worked very hard to live down the violence of our origins. We've tried to save lives and make the world better any way we can. We may not be your children, but we hope that the good that we've done—the lives that we try to lead—will make you proud someday. We're sorry about the horrors of *your* past, but that past won't be your legacy.

"The work you've done, Dr. Skarrstin, *will* be that legacy. Ours is still to come."

Max reached for her face. She didn't flinch as he touched the bruise on the side of her head. He concentrated for a moment, feeling the power moving gently through his body. He watched as the swelling and discoloration lessened, then faded away entirely.

He smiled at her as she touched the spot where the bruise had been, a look of unabashed wonder on her face.

Then he turned and followed his friends down the stairs and out into the hot desert air.

Alone in the upstairs sanctum of her town house, Jolene Skarrstin listened as the three teenagers walked down the stairs and let themselves out. Had they been telling her the truth? Hadn't one of them literally *shown* her the truth? She wasn't sure, even now. She knew she couldn't risk believing, for the sake of the Mortons.

But she knew that she would give her friends the alien teens' message. She would do at least that much for them. Because she wanted very much to believe at least some of what they had told her. Even if the implications were bittersweet.

I have a daughter. I have a grandson.

She crumpled to the floor, weeping. *But they're both light-years away from me.*

19

Jeff Parker delivered a final plate of Will Smith Burgers, Moon Rock Hash, Orbit Rings, and Men in Black-Berry Pie to the tables the group had pushed together. "Will there be anything else, or can I shut down the grill before you kids eat me out of all my inventory?"

Liz stood and hugged her father. "No, thanks, Dad. You and Mom go upstairs and do . . . well, whatever you do when we're not around. We need to do some more . . ."

"Teen talk?" her father offered.

Liz tried not to giggle as Maria made a face like she had just eaten a lemon, and Kyle rolled his eyes. "Yeah, Daddy. Teen talk."

She waited until he had exited the café through the swinging door, then peeked through the crack to make sure he had truly gone upstairs. Returning to the table, she popped Kyle on the head.

"Ow! What was *that* for?" he asked.

"For rolling your eyes at my dad."

"He was being corny," Kyle protested.

Isabel looked sideways at him, her face registering exaggerated shock. "This from the Zen Master?"

"Okay, so finish the story, Maxwell," Maria said, leaning over to grab an Orbit Ring. She put several on Michael's plate as well, and admonished him, "if *I'm* gonna have onion breath, so are *you*."

"Well, after Kyle heroically subdued the sixty-year-old woman who knocked him out—"

"Hey, she caught me by *surprise!*" Kyle protested, chagrined.

"Anyhow, Isabel dreamwalked her, and revealed a bunch of stuff to her about us."

"So now *she* knows you're aliens too?" Maria asked, her mouth open. "Why don't you hire a publicist? Then you won't have to tell folks your secret one at a time."

"Right," said Max, shrugging.

"Oh, I *know* you didn't just *shrug,* Maxwell," Maria said, putting her hand up palm out toward Max. "We go to all the trouble of protecting your secret identities just so Isabel can dreamwalk her and tell her the truth?"

"We needed her to trust us," Isabel said, putting down her Meteor Shower Malt. Liz watched Isabel discreetly add a hefty quantity of Tabasco sauce to it now that Jeff Parker had left.

"Besides, Skarrstin's spent too much of her life hiding from aliens to ever start going after them," Kyle added. "I doubt she's going to be stalking any of you Pod Squadders."

"So what did you get out the trip to Santa Fe?" Michael asked. "Was she able to tell you anything that might help us?"

"Not really," Max said. "She wouldn't tell us where the Mortons are. But I asked her to tell them about us, and apologized for everything she and all of our human templates suffered during their abductions."

"Did you leave the Gandarium with her?" Liz asked, concern in her voice.

"Yeah. *She* knew more about it than *we* do. And I think she'll end up doing some good with it in the long run."

"You've got a lot of faith in someone you just met," Liz said. "Especially someone who looks so much like . . ." She didn't finish the sentence. She didn't need to.

Max took Liz's hand in his. "She's *not* Tess. She never was Tess. She's more like . . . Tess's mother. Only Jolene Skarrstin never got to raise her child. Maybe if she *had* raised Tess, she wouldn't have turned out as bad as she did."

Liz decided to let the matter drop. What mattered was that they were all safe.

"I think she'll *eventually* tell us," Isabel said.

"How will she find you?" Kyle asked.

Isabel tapped her forehead. "I'll keep in touch with her by dreamwalking. Not very often. Just once every now and then."

Max leaned forward to look at Michael, who was sitting on the other side of Maria. "So, it sounds like everything went okay for you in court today."

"Yeah, I guess," Michael said, shrugging. Maria grabbed him by the ear and pinched him, prompting him to quickly amend his statement. "Ow! I mean that it went great. I think they're finally off my back, and it was really nice to have everyone there rooting for me." He saw Isabel frown, and added, "Everyone who was in town, that is."

"So, was Jesse *great*?" Isabel asked, perking up. She saw them all turn to stare at her, and she sipped her shake demurely, and then added, "Well, I mean, he's a good addition to the firm and all. Was his performance in court good?"

"Yeah, after he got over his habit of looking down his nose at me, he did a pretty good job," Michael said, conceding.

Kyle got an evil grin. "Someone's got a crush on the new lawyer. Oooh, Isabel, he's such a *hottie!*" He started to tickle her.

She squirmed away and pointed at him, speaking in a stern tone. "Kyle, don't you dare tickle me, or I'll tell everyone about your little flirtation with the desk clerk."

Kyle immediately withdrew his hands, busying them instead with a slice of Men in Black-Berry Pie.

Liz wasn't sure she wanted to ask the question, but decided to do so anyhow. "This is kind of awkward, but none of us have really talked about it. Michael, how do you feel about Hank's death?"

Everyone looked to Michael for his reaction.

He calmly ate an Orbit Ring, betraying little emotion as he answered in a slightly snooty British accent. "Why, thanks for *asking*, Liz Buzzkill. Not that it's a *touchy* subject or anything."

Liz groaned. "I'm sorry, I just—"

"It's okay," Michael said. "Everyone's probably been asking the same question in their heads anyhow. And at the risk of sounding like one of those *South Park* episodes with 'We've all learned something here today,' I can honestly say that I *have* learned something.

"I feel bad that Hank is dead, and I'm not happy that a certain someone-who-is-no-longer-with-us probably did it. That being said, one of the things that'll keep me snuggly warm as I sleep tonight is knowing that I can beat him in the end. My past on Antar didn't make me what I am. Charles Dupree didn't make me what I am. Nasedo didn't make me what I am. And certainly, Hank Whitmore didn't make me what I am."

He paused long enough to put another Orbit Ring into his mouth. "For better or worse, *I'm* the one who determines my future."

"When I dreamwalked Dr. Skarrstin," Isabel said, "I saw a gallery of portraits of people who looked a lot like me, Max, Michael, and Tess. A few of the pictures looked unfinished. I think now I'm beginning to understand why. Finishing the paintings is up to us."

Everyone seated around the table sat in contemplative silence. Suddenly, Michael pointed over toward Isabel. "Would you pass the Tabasco sauce, alien wench?"

The moment was further broken by a sharp rap on the window of the Crashdown Café. Everyone turned and looked to see Jim Valenti and Amy DeLuca standing outside, holding hands in the clear summer night air. They both waved.

Liz got up and gestured with her arms as if inviting the couple to join them inside, but Valenti waved and mouthed, "No, thanks." The two adults moved on, but Liz caught Michael giving Valenti a thumbs-up sign before he was out of view.

"Ah, young love," said Isabel. "Nice to see they're still dating. It's *sweet*."

Maria blanched and leaned forward, her eyes wide. "Sweet? It's . . . *ewww*! I have to live with the thought of two *old* people . . . doing it in my own house. What is this world coming to?" She shuddered theatrically.

Michael shoved an Orbit Ring into her face so quickly that she had to open her mouth to avoid having the food smooshed against her lips. "You could do a lot worse for a stepdad, Maria," he said as she chewed.

Kyle grabbed the hot sauce bottle. "No more Tabasco for you, mister. That's some *crazy* talk there."

"Why?" Liz asked, laughing.

"Because if my dad and Amy got together and married, that would make me and Maria *stepbrother* and *stepsister*," Kyle said. Smiling broadly, he pointed the bottle at Michael and added, "And I'm not sure I'd approve of an *alien* dating my sister."

The six teens began to laugh, filling the Crashdown Café with the joyous abandon of youth.

ABOUT THE AUTHORS

Andy Mangels is the co-author of *Star Trek: The Next Generation Section 31—Rogue*, *Star Trek: Deep Space Nine Mission: Gamma—Cathedral*, and several future *Star Trek* book projects. Flying solo, he is also the author of the upcoming *Animation on DVD: The Ultimate Guide*, as well as the best-selling book *Star Wars: The Essential Guide To Characters*, plus *Beyond Mulder & Scully: The Mysterious Characters of The X-Files* and *From Scream To Dawson's Creek: The Phenomenal Career of Kevin Williamson.*

Mangels has written for *The Hollywood Reporter, The Advocate, Just Out, Cinescape, Gauntlet, Dreamwatch, Sci-Fi Universe, SFX, Anime Invasion, Outweek, Frontiers, Portland Mercury, Comics Buyer's Guide,* and scores of other entertainment and lifestyle magazines. He has also written licensed material based on properties by Lucasfilm, Paramount, New Line Cinema, Universal Studios, Warner Bros., Microsoft, Abrams-Gentile, and Platinum Studios. His comic-book work has been seen from DC Comics, Marvel Comics, Dark Horse, Wildstorm, Image, Innovation, WaRP Graphics,

Topps, and others, and he was the editor of the award-winning *Gay Comics* anthology for eight years. He is now editing a new anthology, *Gay, Ink.*

In what little spare time he has, he likes to country dance and collect uniforms and Wonder Woman memorabilia. He lives in Portland, Oregon, with his longtime partner, Don Hood.

Visit his Web site at *www.andymangels.com*

Michael A. Martin, whose short fiction has appeared in *The Magazine of Fantasy & Science Fiction*, is co-author of *Star Trek: The Next Generation Section 31—Rogue* and *Star Trek: Deep Space Nine Mission: Gamma—Cathedral* (both with Andy Mangels). Martin was the regular co-writer (also with Andy Mangels) of Marvel Comics' monthly *Star Trek: Deep Space Nine* comic-book series, and has generated heaps of copy for Atlas Editions' *Star Trek Universe* subscription card series. He has written for *Star Trek Monthly, Dreamwatch,* Grolier Books, Wildstorm, Platinum Studios, and Gareth Stevens, Inc., for whom he has penned several *Almanac of the States* nonfiction books. Martin and Mangels currently have several more collaborative projects in the works, including two *Star Trek* novels involving the crew of the *U.S.S. Excelsior* and a *Starfleet Corps of Engineers* e-book.

When not hunkered over a keyboard in his windowless basement, Martin reads voraciously, plots the revolution, and plays with his two sons, James and William. He lives in Portland, Oregon with his wife, Jennifer J. Dottery, their aforementioned children, and a mortgage of galactic proportions.

"Well, we could grind our
enemies into powder with a
sledgehammer, but gosh,
we did that last night."

—Xander

As long as there have been vampires,
there has been the Slayer. One girl
in all the world, to find them where
they gather and to stop the spread of
their evil...the swell of their numbers.

LOOK FOR A NEW TITLE
EVERY MONTH!

Based on the hit TV series created by
Joss Whedon

2400

Everyone's got his demons....

ANGEL™

If it takes an eternity, he will make amends.

Original stories based
on the TV show
Created by Joss Whedon
& David Greenwalt

Available from Simon Pulse
Published by Simon & Schuster

SIMON
PULSE

BASED ON THE HIT TV SERIES

Prue, Piper, and Phoebe Halliwell
didn't think the magical incantation
would really work. But it did.
Now Prue can move things with her
mind, Piper can freeze time, and
Phoebe can see the future. They are
the most powerful of witches—
the Charmed Ones.

Available from Simon & Schuster

I'm 16,
I'm a witch,
and I still have
to go to school?

Look for a new title
every month
Based on the hit TV series

Available from Simon Pulse
Published by Simon & Schuster

. . . A GIRL BORN
WITHOUT THE FEAR GENE

FEARLESS™

A SERIES BY
FRANCINE PASCAL

SIMON
PULSE

FROM SIMON PULSE
PUBLISHED BY SIMON & SCHUSTER

3029